WHAT OTHERS ARE SAYING ABOUT
CHARLIE

"The work has liveliness, originality and great charm. The voice and unique perspective of Charlie will stay in my mind for a long time . . . . The authors made Charlie come alive in my imagination. I felt his plight when boxed-up and left behind and his joy at finding love. The authors have created a memorable and beautiful work."

        Shaun O'Connell, *Remarkable, Unspeakable New York; Imagining Boston: A Literary Landscape*

"This joint venture does wonders for the reader. All he or she needs to bring to *A Bear Called Charlie, A Memoir*, is what every reader of fiction is called on to provide: a willingness to collaborate with the characters, and an imagination free and open enough to be touched by wonder."

        Barry Knister, *Just Bill*

"*Charlie* is a wonderful book, reminiscent of an updated version of A.A. Milne's stories, with overtones of pathos and humor right out of 'Harvey,' the movie wherein Jimmy Stewart converses with a 10-foot invisible rabbit. Beautifully crafted, it's a story that can be read to youngsters, and enjoyed by adults old enough to remember a time when America seemed like a beautiful dream."

        Alan Bisbort, syndicated columnist and author of *Media Scandals; Beatniks*

a bear called
CHARLIE
a memoir

a bear called

CHARLIE

a memoir

ISABEL CRANE GOLDBERG
&
PEG GOLDBERG LONGSTRETH

GOLD MOUNTAIN PRESS

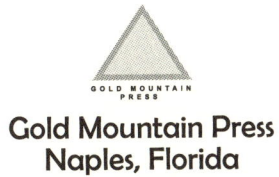

Gold Mountain Press
Naples, Florida

Published By:
Gold Mountain Press

© 2008 by Peg Goldberg Longstreth
All Rights Reserved.
No part of this book may be reproduced, scanned or distributed in any printed or electronic form without permission.

Printed in the United States of America
Cover Graphic Design: TCA Graphics
Photography: Peg Goldberg Longstreth

ISBN: 978-0-9821588-1-4

First Edition

11 10 09 08   1 2 3 4 5

Gold Mountain Press
5640 Taylor Road, Suite D4
Naples, Florida 34109

To learn more about **Charlie** *or*
to purchase additional books, please visit:
www.goldmountainpress.com or
www.charliethebear.com

We're all just children, really, until something happens to shock us right into adulthood . . . . I believe the best of each of us is the child inside, the person we were meant to be, before the world interfered with our innocence.

Charlotte Vale-Allen, ***Painted Lives***

A percentage of the proceeds of each book will be donated to spay-neuter programs and animal rescue organizations.

DEDICATION

This book is dedicated to Big Boy Cat, to Goldie, Foosh, Patches, Herkie, Shawn, Shawna, Scamp, Moira, Tara, Dart, Snippet, Feathers, Louise, Treacle, Myrrh, Jasmine, Randolph Tillsworth, PittiSing, Crackers, the BBC, Miss Biddie, Carmel Dean, Muffin Louise, Pooh Too, Joshua, Willow, Vickie, Smoky Tail Snowball, Blackie White Foots, Sammy Siamese, Chumley the Magnificent – and to my husband, Walter, and daughters, Peg and Madi, who loved them all.

When we learn to be as wise as the animals, we may become human again.

Isabel Crane Goldberg

PROLOGUE

Charlie thought he'd been in that box forever. Cold and lonely in Grandmother's dark attic, he longed for his old life and family. Most of all he missed Sally. He thought he just might be the loneliest teddy bear in the whole world.

He could hear birds singing out in the sun and on the roof overhead, but all he could see in the dim light were the same old pieces of furniture and the stacked boxes from Sally's home, still taped from their move to be stored in the attic.

How Sally cried when she told him goodbye, and how he wanted to cry too. But HIS tears never rolled down his furry cheeks; they just ran down inside, and into his stomach.

The first time I saw Charlie, I almost didn't, for he was nearly at the bottom of a box at an auction. When I picked him up and gazed into his golden eyes, something magical passed between us.

Old and time-worn (from a lot of past loving, I hoped), dressed in a wrinkled, pink-checked gingham dress, his gold eyes gazed at me and, coupled with his determined, stalwart chin, I thought, "Shoot! This teddy bear's a **boy**! What's he doing in this dumb doll dress?"

Had I only known the range of emotions which were to come from my frustration at trying to piece his story together, had I known the chaos that would go on in our home for several years as I helped him write his story – I'd have left that auction and never looked back. (No sooner have I written this, than I feel as guilty as if I'd denied the existence of my children!)

I expect that's been my problem in trying to help Charlie write his story: I can't avoid thinking him human.

Ultimately I had no choice but to take a hard look at my life. Some changes would have to be made to make time to help Charlie write his story. My chronic disorganization, my trying to gulp all of life's enchantments, swallow them whole – but finish so few (also chronic). Writing his story became the driving force in my life, and necessitated either finishing or discarding most other projects I'd started.

Hard choices.

But I looked at Charlie just as he looked at me with those gold eyes and I knew which choice I would make.

> *When was the last time I saw Sally? Charlie wondered. Somebody, one time, said it was about fifty years ago, but who said it, and why can't I count? Numbers seem to mean a lot to people, but nobody's ever had time to help me learn.*
>
> *I remember some of my ABCs though: A is for Apple, B is for Box, Sally said. Well, I sure know about boxes, but the people who named them didn't know what it was like to be shut in one for a hundred and ten years! Or was that the "fifty years" stuff?*
>
> *Memories flooded back as Charlie remembered the day Sally and her mother came to the Army post shop where Sally was to choose her birthday present. Sally had squealed and pointed, and begged her mother . . . "Please! Can I have that bear right there?"*
>
> *And so Charlie, brand new from the factory, clean golden fur on his head and paws and dressed in a uniform like Sally's dad and the other soldiers, went happily into the arms of his first mother.*
>
> *My nice uniform's gone now, though, he sighed, as he looked down at the tatters and saw his legs showing. And there's my old black feet! Wonder why that manufacturing-bird didn't finish my body with fur like my head and paws? Sally's mother said one*

time, she 'spected it being war time, and all the good stuff going into the **WAR EFFORT***, he just didn't have enough fur. You know what* **I** *think, though? I think he was a real "cheepie" and saw a way to make a fast buck.*

Oh well; too late now, but I wish my shiny boots hadn't melted like the candle did on poor Squirrely's tail . . . . What a mess!

It sure gets hot up here. I guess that's what they call Summer. Wonder how many of those Summer-things have gone by since I landed here?

At the sale, my hurried examination of the other items came to a sudden halt as I heard the auctioneer's first call for a bid, and I quickly unfolded my chair, sat down, and gave him my full attention. I thought of the second cup of tea I hadn't had time for in my hurried breakfast, but was afraid to leave my chair. Instead, I settled for a stale candy bar I found in the depths of my disorganized purse. I sat back and listened with my usual amazement at the money people were willing to spend on boxes of junk.

Had I overlooked something fantastic? What had they seen that **I'd** missed? Questions flew through my head. Ah! The lure of hidden treasure at an auction!

I hoped there would be few bidders on "my" box, but with the gone-to-the-moon-prices for even the most dilapidated teddies, I wasn't too surprised when the bids began to rise alarmingly. Maybe the aggressive expression on my face helped discourage other bidders for, as I'd call a bid and look around, some of them dropped out. (Father – that is what I call my husband – says I can look pretty fierce when I set my mind on something, but I picture myself as a pretty laid-back old lady with kind blue eyes and, most times, a pleasant smile). But then, maybe I do have my moments.

My pulse raced as I called out my absolute limit, and then was shocked when I realized what I had paid for this collection of unfinished quilt pieces, a pathetic stuffed squirrel huddled next to the bear, one or two fairly choice Christmas ornaments, and a bent egg beater! But – there was the bear. He was mine!

Thankfully, I had to forego bidding on other desirable items. Father wouldn't have to shuffle some things in order to make room for another acquisition. Surely he would be pleased.

I put my box in a safe place close to the clerk's desk, then grabbed a cup of hot tea before starting home. Snow was coming down again, and I was a little apprehensive about the drive. I remembered then that I needed to stop at the market, where an advertised bargain on peaches had led to the trip to the auction. I'd used those peaches as an excuse to get out of the house and do something sensible.

But now the day held another surprise, for after settling with the clerk and hurrying over to get my bear, **NO BEAR WAS IN MY BOX**!

"Good Heavens!" I said, louder than I'd meant and, as I began to examine other boxes, I could see the suspicious look on the clerk's face. So, while babbling inanely about how easy it is to get confused . . . so many boxes look alike . . . and on and on, still trying to keep my composure and look businesslike, I frantically lifted corners and peered into nearby boxes. Suddenly, I spied one golden eye and one alert golden ear in the corner of an unfamiliar box.

"Well, gee!" I exclaimed. "I guess I've been looking in the wrong box. Dumb me!"

I could have sworn I felt the bear smile when I trundled him and all my other new prized possessions off to the car and headed home that afternoon.

Do you know how lonely it is to be stuck in a cardboard box in a dark attic for fifty years?

Why couldn't anybody tell I was a BOY bear before my Mom rescued me at that dreadful auction, for gosh sakes!

1

CHARLIE MOVES IN . . . TO MY HEART

I don't know exactly when writing Charlie's story became an obsession.

Certainly the day I bought him was no red-letter-day. Of course, I was glad I'd outbid others, who for hours had hovered over the box of odds-and-ends in which poor Charlie had found himself. But one of my worst (or best) attributes is tenacity. Maybe not finishing projects, but hanging in there. Those bidders should have sensed that!

And so Charlie came home with me. But then some explaining was needed for my husband, Father wondering why, with all the fascinating items on the long sales-bill, I had brought home only this slightly worn, unremarkable old teddy bear? I hoped Charlie hadn't sensed Father's disenchantment. He looked woebegone enough already. I hurried to my room to place him lovingly on the only available surface – a chair – and went to prepare our belated supper.

I believe the big difference between Father and me in our perception of this old teddy bear was that he had not really looked into Charlie's golden eyes. For it was the eyes that did it at the sale. Certainly not that old, faded pink checked gingham dress. Not the fact that I might have something of a bargain, for although his price hadn't been that low, still a lot of people have gone more-or-less bananas in acquiring teddy bears, and their prices are astronomical sometimes.

I hadn't perceived at first just what it was about those eyes of Charlie's, but evidently they reached into some void I hadn't even known was there. Some time later, Charlie pointed out to me that he thought my acquiring such an enormous gathering of toy friends (which reside in my room) may be because I subconsciously endow them with desirable human characteristics . . . substitute them for humans who may have disappointed me. (At the time it was just a fleeting thought which passed between Charlie and me.)

I don't expect you to believe that Charlie talks. That would destroy whatever credibility I may have built between us so far. But there **IS** something which passes between us when we sit and look at one another, and I can't put it into words any better than with that simple statement.

As my friendship with Charlie grew over several months, I decided that many of us need an entity with whom we can let down the barriers of normalcy which guide our lives. That, being unsure of how people are going to react to some statement or act of ours, we search for this some one with whom we can be completely honest and not worry about how we will be perceived. Or measure us against some "normal" yardstick.

And I believe that's what I found in Charlie: a completely receptive, uncritical acceptance of me – just the way I am.

So Charlie found himself that first snowy evening in his new home, being unwrapped from a blanket I carry in the car to protect some new, breakable thing I've purchased at an auction. Unwrapped, then re-wrapped expediently in a piece of warm, brown wool blanket I'd salvaged from – what else? – another auction. Not that it was cold in our room, but he looked so forlorn and mis-placed, I thought the reassurance of this security blanket would be just right. So I draped it around him and pinned it with an antique Scottish-thistle pin at one shoulder to cover that awful pink-checked dress. I could tell he felt embarrassed!

The piece of blanket added just a fraction to this scenario which was, unbeknownst to me, already building in my mind. And coupling it with the Scottish-thistle pin seemed appropriate, for the blanket had been Woven in Scotland, its label said, and that's the reason I had bought it in the first place. I'm just beginning to research my Scots ancestry, but having so little time, or expertise for logical organization of my ancestors, over the past several years I guess I've accumulated a mouse-nest pile of things pertaining to Scotland!

I thought vaguely then about finding some suitable material to make Charlie more presentable. Tartan? But as the weeks rolled along, I'm ashamed to admit I sort of forgot about Charlie. I'd give him a passing glance as he stood on his chair with "Big Red" bear and two or three other furry personages, then hurry on to do something pressing.

And there was always something pressing. Unfinished. Running-behind-on. I guess I've always tried to do too many things. But as I've grown older and slower and, of necessity more selective, some of the things I'd thought so important a few years ago had been eliminated before Charlie came to live with us.

But though my looms were gone, my paintings put aside, now very unexpectedly writing Charlie's story took over my life (or what was left of it)! And this presented a big problem: Just how was I going to find time for writing?

A partial solution came suddenly as I belatedly realized now that having just one focus – to write Charlie's story – was a blessing. Did it take Charlie to make me see this? Truthfully, I don't know.

Then the most important gift of all – time – came to me when Father finally decided to retire. And surprisingly, for I would have supposed he'd consider it beneath his dignity to become involved in mundane household processes after years of an important financial career. He even seemed to enjoy the routine chores I'd begun to resent. And, as he saw how important this new endeavor was to me, he just stepped in unselfishly and took over.

Well, naturally, there were a few glitches. But I had Charlie for a safety-valve when, for instance, familiar layouts in each room were re-organized and **I** wasn't; and I soon learned a familiar tool in its once familiar place had also been re-organized. Methodically. All neat. Tidy. In the basement now!

But how gladly I accepted these precious hours Father gave me. I'd sit, maybe all day, typing madly. Thinking I'd had it, then finding I didn't. Being very discouraged. Being en-couraged then by Father, who pointed out, kindly, that I hadn't had any experience.

The strangest thing in those first two years of this new cockeyed routine, was that I couldn't let go of *"Charlie,"* for he sounded so clear! I heard his voice all the time, but I was having such a hard time getting him down on paper. I realize now this was because I was using my words to transform him into my ideas of what his story should sound like!

Evidently Charlie'd never written a book either, so he didn't realize what a muddle he was getting me into as he reeled off long expositions. And then something in what he'd said would remind him of something else – and away he'd go on that! I finally decided that all those long, abandoned years in an attic had filled his head to overflowing with things he'd never been able to say 'til now.

All this time, while I'd been trying to re-organize myself, I found methodical Father was changing the pattern of our living. Providentially, though, he began to be intrigued by Charlie, although they never established the complete rapport that Charlie and **I** had. And Charlie complained to me several times that Father talked to the cats a lot, but hadn't said much to him.

But I told him a dignified, elderly male might think it pretty embarrassing if someone heard him conversing with a teddy bear. Charlie answered me right back, saying he didn't see why that was true: hadn't some of his conversations with me seemed pretty normal? I changed the subject.

But sadly, I will never know what might have evolved between Father and Charlie, for disaster struck on a chilly January afternoon and, after a seemingly routine repair of a broken hip, Father slipped quietly away one May morning.

Never complaining. Just gone.

As the months turned into a year, and I tried to reorganize, there were times when I knew Father must be helping us make important decisions. There were a lot of things we'd know the answer to someday.

During all these months, not a word came from Charlie. I must confess that a few fleeting daydreams of "The Book" crossed my mind as I looked at my furry friends collected through the years. But they were now just toys, almost a nuisance, having to be kept tidy with the feather duster, sitting silently, waiting.

Finally, into the long bride's chest they were moved, and several of them went to needy children that first empty, Fatherless Christmas.

Trivial things, unnecessary-to-survival things, and for months the laboriously written chapters of Charlie's book fell into this same category. But then one day, as I desperately searched for yet another something, I sat looking at Charlie. I thought of the many things Father had done so that I could have time to write. Thought of how pleased he had been that I was creating something good, and comforting, and satisfying – something I **was** going to finish!

As I gazed at Charlie I saw, as always, his steadfast, reassuring expression. And we began to write. Ideas which had lain dormant suddenly appeared, the words spilling out. Not always easily, but appearing from somewhere. Charlie's voice.

From the threads of understanding – words which bind us all together if we but listen with our hearts – a skein of comfort magically spun its way onto the pages.

"Bear ye one another's burdens?" Charlie asked. *"Is that what you've been trying to say?"*

2

THE BEAR ESSENTIALS: CHARLIE BEGINS TO WRITE

When I woke up early this morning, I was absolutely **determinated** I **was** going to help Mom finalize the beginning of my story. You don't know how many months (and I don't either, since I can't count very far yet) Mom and I have tried to write my book.

A v-e-r-y long time. Mom says maybe nearly five years. All the rest of my story's done, but you know what I think has been our hangup in this first chapter? Trying to explain just how come a teddy bear turns out to be the author of a book!

But I said this morning something like, "well, Mom, if they're true arctophiles, (i.e. bear lovers), they're gonna already know that almost anything can happen between an understanding bear and his family, aren't they?"

After a few moments of thought, or maybe that was some kind of a human-nap Mom was having because she hadn't had her third cup of T, she agreed with me. And so we decided that about all that was necessary to introduce this book was just the **bear** essentials. OK?

So, first of all, I guess I'm maybe an "almost anteek" teddy bear, for I was stuffed about fifty years in a box in an attic and was pretty much out of touch with the world. So it's been really hard for me to adjust to this new life that Mom rescued me into. (And right here, she says something about "dangling participles," but if I get into what she calls English Composition, I never **will** get this done). Anyway, after Mom rescued me at that gruesome sale, I came home with her — thankfully to a nice, warm, loving environment.

Now, besides my Mom, there's Father, who's recently retired from some kind of weighty financial-stuff, and trying to adjust to a wife he thought he knew. But she's off and running now, trying to write my life story. We don't know why she wants to do this, but in Father's patient way he's accepted what he calls the "inevitable," and tries to help our house go on running.

Obsessed. I think that's what Father called it one morning, when he saw the dishes left unwashed, the cats not fed, and several other things he used to figure sort of automatically got done. By whom? Now, by Father, and this way Mom and I have a lot of time to write.

There are also two pretty ancient cats in our home: one female Siamese, one golden Tabby, both rescued, who, in my opinion should know better than to continually sniff at me when Mom forgets to close the door to our room. I do know I'm not edible, and they're overstuffed anyway! But I'll not criticize the cats. They've lived here most all their fifteen-plus years, and I'm just the new kid on the block.

Well, here I was on this chair where Mom put me, next to a bear called Big Red. I looked all around that first night and wondered what on earth my life was going to be like here in my new home. How could I have known what a disruptive influence I was going to be? I don't believe anybody did right at first, for it was a good many months later that this writing bug bit Mom.

Why, I don't know. Nobody seemed to have the remotest notion why this was happening. But, suddenly, here she was, going around talking to herself. I have a heck of a time some days, figuring out when she needs an answer to some question. All this talking seemed to be focused on trying out scenarios. Not liking most of them; **not being able to get Charlie down on paper**!

Aggravated, disappointed in herself, maybe she'd bitten off more than she could chew. She'd be explaining this to Father, and I guess to friends who were sympathetic, but they couldn't solve this either. Although that's what friends are for, aren't they? So they tried to help, and one night at some sort of a writers'-meeting-thing, this brilliant, female-writer-person said to Mom, "Why don't you let Charlie tell his own story?"

Simple question, right? Why didn't **Mom** think of it? Why didn't I think of it?

Are you kidding? I was more shook up than Mom. Me writing a book was about the very farthest thing from anywhere I'd ever thought about.

Even after that, lots of well-meant plans fell through the cracks. Like "getting me down on tape." **Nothing** when Mom played it back on that awesome RADIO/ALARMED-CLOCK/TAPE RECORDER-PLAYER thing which, even after three or four years, she still hasn't learned to work. (She got put down in the wrong century, I think). And I'll never forget the look on her face when she turned around and looked at me, stunned. "Absolutely zilch," she said. "Just my Midwest-Hoosier twang! I cannot believe it, Charlie! Not a single word you told me."

But I would have thought Mom would have known by then that I never give voice-interviews! Well . . . after she sat for awhile, thinking about things, she pulled herself together. And she said something about using the tapes to record a symphony or something inspiring. "Waste not, want not, Charlie," she said, and seemed to feel better.

Mom's staring-into-space thing went on for awhile, but suddenly a warm, sort of satisfied smile lit up her face, and she said: "What a great idea, Charlie! You're going to write your own story!"

So it looks like I have no choice. Besides, it's sort of flattering that my Mom has this much confidence in me. Maybe I just needed a shove in the right direction.

Just to have somebody believe in you is pretty wonderful, I think.

3

LEFT BEHIND: LIVING IN A BOX

Mom and I talk a lot while I'm trying to write this book. (I really think maybe I should call her "Mother," but some way that doesn't seem right: maybe it sounds too dignified for my "Mom.")

I never knew my real mother. I was borned during the 1940s War, in a toy factory with a lot of other bears. And some of us — times being what they were right then, with all the good stuff going to The War Effort — some of us ended up with not enough fur. That's the reason only my gorgeous head and beautiful golden paws are mohair. (I really hate to say this out loud) my body's red flannel, and my feet are old black cloth!

But I refuse to feel pathetic about that. Life's full of little disappointments, I know, and I'll take what I was dealt all those years ago. Mom says I just need to be philosophical about this, for more than likely that manufacturer really didn't have enough mohair, and did his best.

I have my own private opinion about that whole bit, though, and this is what **I** think: I think my manufacturer was a real "cheepie." Here were all these stressed-out wartime parents, trying to find something to take their kids' minds off all the awful things like a war going on, and Ration Cards for food, and so forth. And so this man sneaked me in a uniform like all the soldiers were wearing, and covered up my red-flannel body!

Neat, huh? Who's gonna look under that uniform? And after they look into my golden, appealing, spellbinding eyes (I hate to mention that, but Mom says that's what she calls them), who's gonna care that my body's made of old red flannel?

Anyway, not long after I went from the factory to a toy shop on this Army post, a dear little girl by the name of Sally fell in love with me, and her mother bought me and took me home to live with them.

It's pretty hard for me to tell you about those first things I remember, but there was a lot of happiness there. Sally and I found a lot of things to do, and we really loved one another. I wasn't too fond of some of the things that went on, though. Every once in a while something called "orders" would come in, and there'd be this awful tension around our house until the names of the men who were being shipped out would be posted.

But Sally and I lived in our own little world, I guess. And even if I wasn't too crazy about her little brother, who had a bad habit of picking me up by my tender ears every once in a while, still things were really warm and wonderful for those first few months.

Then one day the roof fell in! A lot of crying began in our house, and I didn't know what was wrong. But I knew it was pretty devastating, for Sally'd take me to bed with her now, and most nights she'd cry herself to sleep. I couldn't do one thing about that, though, for my tears never come out my eyes – they just run down inside, into my stomach. (Mom says she thinks there are a lot of people just like me, probably, for they don't dare let their tears outside either, but just "bottle them up inside.")

But I haven't figured that out.

Anyway, one morning before I knew it, real bad things happened, and our life began to fall apart. As near as I could figure out, my family was going to have to move. And Sally's mother was going to work in a factory, while Sally's father got shipped out to somewhere where lots of people were fighting over something or other.

All our things began to be put in big boxes, to be stored in Sally's grandmother's attic, while what was left of my family moved way off someplace where they'd be able to live until the government checks started to come in.

Pictures, and dishes, and all the things began to disappear, to go into these big boxes, and I sat there watching. And then – I could not believe it – **I** went into a box too! But Sally hugged me tight and told me it wouldn't be long til she'd come and get me, but – and I can hardly tell you this – I never saw her again! And I thought for years, whenever I heard somebody coming up the stairs to the attic where I lived in my box – I'll bet that's Sally!

It never was.

So I settled down to the inevitability of the matter. That's Mom's phrase, and I guess it is better than whatever I'd come up with right now. I just noticed there's some more tears running down to my insides and I'd better stop and pull myself together before I try to go on.

4

GOLDEN THREADS: TIES THAT BIND

When I get to looking back over my years in Grandmother's attic, I guess it wasn't all bad. It gave me a lot of time to think. 'Course I didn't know very much to think about, because I'd lived in this human-world such a short time after my "borning" by this manufacturing-cheepie. But I knew **some** things, like this lonely, lonely feeling.

So I made a solemn promise to myself: to find my Sally!

Some day.

A lot of cold-feeling-times came and went while I was in that box, and I was glad to have on that red-flannel, although I thought manufacturing-cheepie could have made me warmer with mohair. But then sometimes – whew! – it really got hot. And one time a candle in our box melted, and poor Squirrely, who lived next to me among all the other things Sally's mother had packed in there, had this glommy candle-stuff stuck all over his tail.

I felt really sorry for him, but I didn't know what to do about it.

One day, as the seasons came and went, it was so hot, I thought maybe I'd shed my uniform, but I couldn't work the buttons. Pretty soon that took care of itself. The uniform began to come apart, and then I was even colder in the winter.

The worst thing in that box was an egg-beater. Just about the time I'd try to take a nap and get half-way snoozed off, it would poke me! Then one day I noticed some of the quilt-pieces Sally's mother hadn't had time to finish, had candle-wax on them too. When I thought of all her patient stitches, it made me even sadder. And I guess I could have cried, and maybe I did shed a tear or two. But nobody saw them.

Except Squirrely.

Not every last thing was sad; one time Grandmother came up the creaking stairs to find some toys for kids who'd come to visit. Now, by this time my uniform was really falling apart. And – get this! She took this dress off an anteek doll and put it on ME!

Oh gosh! Was I embarrassed! But somehow we'd never been able to communicate. Didn't she know I had a lot of things to tell her? Like I wasn't a girl? I couldn't seem to make her understand, though, so I just gave up and wore that dress. Besides, was it ever great to get out of that box!

So, here I was in that old pink-checked gingham dress, and I guess somebody'd spent a lot of time sewing it. It had lace around the neck and a little pocket with a funny gold button-thing in it, which was going to play an important part in my life much later.

Grandmother took me downstairs, and there I sat in my worn finery that afternoon, at a little T-party-thing with these little girls. Drinking T. (At least that's what they called it: "T.") And they chattered away in some sort of make-believe-world, and things were pretty nice. Except for the T. And the fact that they thought I was a girl!

Finally, here was a chance for me to talk, and I had a lot of stories I'd heard on the Army post, and I thought maybe I'd tell some of them. But there were some funny sounding words in the stories that the soldiers really laughed about, and I didn't know what they meant, so I decided I'd just let my end of the conversation lag and sat there — just being a highly appealing bear, hoping they'd notice.

But the afternoon ended, and away I went . . . right back into the box! I couldn't believe it! Why hadn't somebody seen what a super addition I'd make to their household?

It took my Mom to see that.

Mom told me how she'd been fascinated with anteek auctions for years and years. She said she guessed she "caught the bug from her dad," who added to their farm-income during The Depression by using something she called his horse swapping talents to buy things at a bargain. Then he'd swap or sell them to somebody else for a lot more. She never said anything more about horses, though, so I don't know what **that** had to do with anything.

Then, she said: "When my dad would get home with his bargains, Grandpa Rice (a lovable old cuss, Mom called him) would shake his head and ask why on earth dad was bringing home some more old dishes?" Or: "Hadn't you better save your money to use on equipment, or supplies for the acres of apple orchards we're trying to make a living from?"

But Mom's father had what she called the last laugh, several times: once he even got this $20 gold piece for some sort of an anteek glass wedding jar with a kneeling Indian on top. Sure sounded weird to me, but I guess it shut up her Grandpa for awhile.

Now every once in a while, while we were talking, I'd try to reassure Mom that we were going to get my story all written — someday — if she'd just discipline herself and quit getting off the subject. I might be a "highly intelligent bear" (Mom said that over and over), but that didn't mean I didn't need her help telling my story.

But it sort of seemed to me that, the more we talked, the more confused she became. And every once in a while I'd notice her, just sitting on the edge of the bed she'd started to make, and we'd be talking away, when she'd jump up frantically, saying something about "Lunch! Oh, my! How can it be that time?" And stuff like that.

I don't understand why humans are so worried about time "getting away" when they've got about twenty-six hours every day to do something with. Wonder what happens to it?

I tried my very best to get Mom straightened out on this, but she said something about me being mixed up, that twenty-six had to do with the alphabet letters, not time.

Right here I'm going to have to admit something pretty awful: I don't understand alphabets, and time, and letters in a book, and a lot of things like that. I've mentioned to Mom (I believe more than once) that I think I should be able to read, and to count, and to understand whatever these words mean that she says once in awhile: "To make a proper order of things, all neatly arranged, so that they make some sense."

But she just looks at me sort of sadly, and then tells me she doesn't know of any schools for bears, and stuff like that. One time she said something about betting a lot of teachers felt they'd had a room full of bears at the end of a hard day.

And I didn't know what on earth she meant, so I said, "Is that good or bad?" And she said, "Maybe somewhere in between."

Confusing sometimes. That's Mom.

I am **determined**, though, that I am going to pursue this stuff about reading and writing with all my might! How discriminatory can you get? I don't think that's equal opportunity at all, for bears like me being unable to go to school!

But I started back somewhere to tell you about the sale where Mom rescued me. That was **s-o-m-e** day!

Mom said she'd seen an ad in a newspaper for this great-sounding sale full of anteeks and, besides, in the same paper there'd been an ad for a great bargain on cases of peaches. And Mom, having given up on the hours it takes to peel and can peaches several years ago, on account of having some of them ferment – Mom decided this was a "heaven-sent coincidence!" She'd drive over and pick up the peaches and probably save enough money so that she wouldn't feel too guilty about not staying home and doing useful things; maybe she'd find a real bargain at the sale.

That turned out to be **me**! Mom says there were maybe a thousand people there in the Armory at the sale, all trying to get into the same boxes at the same time. They were in a sort of human frenzy, shoving like a flock of starlings trying to get the same piece of bread.

She said she'd just about decided she'd have to give up and go on home with the peaches (and I really hate to tell you this, but she went home without them after all! Has a bit of a memory-problem sometimes, Mom does). Anyway, in this one box where I was living, she'd rummaged through, dispiritedly – and then she saw me! I was trying my very best to give her a signal, for I thought this was just about my last hope to get out of there. The box, I mean.

Strangely, I wasn't too impressed by Mom at first, and I believe she told me the same thing later: not being impressed by me either. But maybe it was the eyes that "did it" – on both sides I mean. For when I looked into her blue, crinkly-cornered eyes, and then saw the beginnings of a smile turn up the corners of her mouth . . . **O-HO!** I thought! Put on your **VERY BEST** appearance, Charlie!

Of course, there wasn't anything much I could do about appearing special wearing that darned dress. But I gave her such an appealing, steadfast look out of my eyes (which I have to admit are my best feature), that I believe she was hooked! That's what she told me later, but she's never been able to explain what that means, exactly.

I just knew that something passed between us like a golden thread of hope and longing, and began to tie us together, me and Mom.

Well, boy oh boy! How that sale went on and on, Mom sitting there with her bid-number waiting on my box with other people bidding so high on things, I began to get discouraged. The tension got so bad, I just decided I'd take a nap, for I was just about worn out from the trip way off somewhere in a big, roarey truck, not knowing what was going to happen. Thinking, from the condition of the other stuff in my box, that probably the whole schmeer was going to the dump! Including me! So I tried to nap — while I guess Mom really began to get tense, like humans do — but there was that darned egg beater poking me again.

Some time later the box began to move, but I was about half-asleep from the heat and the noise and being so worn out and all, so I only half-sensed it. Mom said later that she was so tired she'd decided to have what she called a "quick cuppa" — and a lovely piece of pie.

As I peeped from the box I saw I was now sitting by a cold, half-open door. In a different box. No Squirrely anywhere in this other box!

There's not much time now to say goodbye to my friend from the attic! I thought suddenly.

But before I could make it back to my box, here came Mom: all in a real dither! Couldn't find her bear . . . wondered if somebody'd pulled a fast one and put me in **their** box. (Which was more or less confirmed when she found me in the other box!) Looking around to see if anyone was watching, then putting me back in **her** box.

Then telling the sales clerk she thought she'd got the wrong box! Beating it out the door, almost running to our car, wondering if there'd be big headlines in the paper about . . . **ELDERLY WOMAN HELD FOR TEDDY BEAR THEFT AT AUCTION!**

Some imagination, that's my mom!

Collapsing in a heap in our cold car after she'd shoved the big carton in the trunk. Then turning on the heater, for it was cold and beginning to snow. Right from the start being really concerned about me: and turning the heater to "high." Wrapping me in a blanket there in the front seat beside her.

And I'll never forget what she said to me with this smile on her face: "If I live to be a hundred and one, and who knows? My family's pretty long-lived...." She looked into my eyes and said to me, out loud, for the very first time: "We'll let the car run just a minute to get warmer. I'll sure be glad to get home. I'm about worn out. Aren't you?"

Right about here, since she'd initiated this conversation, I figured it was appropriate to say just a few words, so I said, "OK! Let's head for home. I'm sick of this place!"

Well, I didn't see any reason for her to look so surprised. After all, she'd started this conversation, so I figured she knew I was an intelligent bear who came with a voice and a lot of other things. So I tried to continue this interesting conversation as we started home.

Every once in a while, she'd look around at me as we went to my new home, and I'd try to get in a few more words. But evidently cars need a lot of attention to keep them on the road, so I'd just get started talking as we'd make eye contact, then she'd be watching the road again, sort of humming to herself.

A little later, I began to feel the car slow down as we turned a corner, and then we were in a driveway and the snow was coming down pretty hard now. Mom turned off the car, gave me her full attention and smiled at me, so I decided it was about time to introduce myself. That way she'd know what to call me in the hopefully long years ahead when we'd be together.

I wiggled my head loose from the blanket, got my chin out far enough to talk, and started: "Hi. In case you're wonderin' about my name, it's Charlie, and I'm sure glad you brought me to live with you. You have, haven't you? You're not just gonna turn around and sell me to somebody to make money 'cause I'm an anteek, are you?"

Just silence, so I went on: "I don't exactly know what an 'anteek' is, but I heard people talking about making money on them, and somebody tried to steal me from your box, so I got worried I might be one. I haven't been able to live outside a box for a long time, and I really would like to have a real home again. Your house looks warm and friendly, and I already can tell I would like to live here."

Evidently this was still unexpected – me talking, I mean, for Mom got this strange, wide-eyed look on her face, tried to smile, grabbed me and ran for the house. She even forgot the rest of the box in the trunk, and when Father found it later and lugged it into the house with a resigned look, she still hadn't remembered she'd put it there!

And Father, systematically looking through the box before he stored it with her other purchases in the big closet downstairs, came across a new, expensive fishing-reel in a little box, clear in the bottom of the carton.

And he said something to her about good things coming in small packages. And she said "Well, don't they now!" Thinking he was talking about me!

But his brown eyes were twinkling, so Mom thought he was happy, and boy, so was I!

Home at last. Me and Mom.

5

THE NITTY GRITTY OF THINGS

Every time we tried to work more on my story, Mom kept getting distracted.

Sometimes when we looked at each other, we knew we were both getting older, and maybe we would run out of time before we finished writing my story. Things, she would say to me lots of times, just keep getting in the way of our plans.

Disorganated, but well intentioned, that's my Mom.

And I'd just sit there quietly. Not ever disagreeing with her about what she was saying about both of us getting distracted by other things. It was my Mom who got distracted, not me. I just sat there, trying to understand everything, mostly doing something I'd heard Father call "taking it all in." After all, although I didn't think Mom had any question but that I was a highly intelligent, well-spoken bear, I **had** been stuffed into a cardboard box in an attic with no light and no real opportunity for conversation for years.

I was just a young bear when Sally, my first mother, got me for her special birthday present. I guess I'd been stuck in that attic so long, I was now an anteek, which I was beginning to understand meant someone or something very old.

As I look back, I know Mom had not known just how universal this mutual love between teddy bears and humans has become since the first teddies began to be made. But it didn't take long after I came to live with Mom before she began to find out this book idea of hers was apparently pretty enormous, for one of Mom's daughters thought so, too (the one Father teasingly calls "Big Sissy" 'cause she's so tall. Really tall. Not at all like her sister or Mom or Father). She brought Mom a magazine **just** for teddy bear lovers! And when she read that there are big conventions just for bear lovers, and when all this sank in, she probably sat down in a heap.

But I really don't know. I was too busy writing.

One day Mom read a newspaper story to me about some woman calling her kids' teddy a "hero," saying, "Now, if I hadn't had to go out in the yard at night to see if the kids had left teddy out in the rain, I never would have seen smoke coming out the roof. The whole house would have burned down!"

And as Mom read to me, I wondered: just what was a **hero**? And what made him a hero, I asked Mom, because I still didn't get it.

"Now, don't worry about that, Charlie. Heroes are born every day and some of them are never recognized for what they've done. You don't have to do some big thing – just be yourself!" (Well, who else would I be? I didn't get that either.) I felt sort of sad, for maybe I wasn't measuring up to something that somebody expected of me.

Then, one afternoon, Mom came home from a recreational meeting with some other older ladies at this food place, and said something about bear-mania being even more widespread than she dreamed!

And I was afraid it was some kind of a **disease** among my friends, and I was really worried!

But Mom explained she'd said something to a friend about writing this book. And the friend took off immediately, telling Mom about her "Bruiser Bear," which she said "is my very best friend!" And Mom said to me that the lady had four kids and a husband, and she sort of wondered how she was so short of friends that she'd made her bear her very best friend.

(Well, I couldn't understand what was questionable about that! After all, I thought I was **Mom's** best friend!)

So I tried to help Mom find time, and outlined my life in stages, and a good many of my chapters accumulated in a sort-of organized pile. But then there would come days when she'd have to forget about me, for about this time some pretty big family responsibilities began to descend which, I guess – me not understanding all these things – **had** to come first.

Suddenly I got very scared. The first time "big family responsibilities" happened in my life, I ended up abandoned, in a cardboard box in a dark attic.

"Oh no, Charlie," Mom exclaimed, hugging me, when she realized why I was upset. "No one's **ever** going to put you in a box in our attic. You're family."

So, once again, I snuggled down on my chair to wait for Mom to be done with this "important family matter," so she could continue helping me write the rest of my book. Mom calls it "my" chair, although to tell you the truth it **is** getting pretty crowded! For one thing, there's this enormous rabbit-person who moved in recently, named "A.B." – which I found out stood for "Abandoned Rabbit." I found out why later. And there's "Big Red" bear, who's lived here for a number of years, but – says Mom suddenly to me – "He's been so lonely, Charlie, I think I'll move him over with you, so you can keep each other company."

And I have a feeling that pretty soon somebody else may move in.

But here I am right now, right where Mom put me that first cold, wonderful night she brought me home. No sooner had she put me down than she went away quickly, and tried to become "a well-organized *hausfrau*." (Put a nice meal on the table, have a serious talk with Father about his pending retirement.) Then they toddled off to bed.

Well, it got pretty cold in my room that night. For some reason, Mom always leaves the window open – it has something to do with "fresh air." I don't really understand that. I thought all air was supposed to be fresh! But I'm getting some pretty pertinent information about air, and trees, and things like that from Big Red, who's sitting there, talking some. He's been a quiet bear most of the time – had almost forgotten how to talk, I guess. Up until I came into Mom's life, I don't believe she ever really talked to him.

Guess she hadn't realized until recently that conversation, in order to flow, has to go two ways.

Anyway, Big Red is pretty smart, and darn – he is the **furriest** thing! And besides that, he's outfitted in a cream-and-crimson Indiana University bear-size wool jacket. He says someone called "The Doll Lady" sewed it for him before Mom adopted him and brought him home. Because he's "such a fan," (whatever that is).

Now, don't get the idea that I'm jealous of B.R. I'm just glad that things worked out pretty good for him when they doled out fur, but I said to Mom that first morning in my new home (when she finally pried her eyes open), that I believed I had the shivers.

"Are you cold?" She asked.

And here came my first good hug! Oh boy! You just have no idea how good that hug felt! All warm and nice, and I could just have stayed there forever, I guess. But about this time Mom, having looked at that darned alarmed-clock thing, and hearing its beginning *brrrg,* reluctantly decided she'd better get with it, and took off for the kitchen.

Mom's really something she calls a "night person;" always has trouble with "morning stuff." I don't really understand that; seems pretty much the same to me. But she worries a lot about Father being something she calls a "morning person," and how cheerful he always is, and something that sounds peculiar to me. She told me his brain seems to be in gear the minute his feet touch the floor.

I don't really understand what that means, but I don't want her to be disappointed with me, and worry I'm not as intelligent as she thought, so I just smile and keep quiet.

She even said to me once she believed I'd inherited something she calls a "gene" of Father's. Now I was really confused; I haven't the remotest idea what she meant, but I think it may be something really good, so I just continue to sit quietly and try to look intelligent.

Well, when she came back, after discovering that morning-person Father had fixed his own breakfast and was happily reading the morning paper, I thought I'd reassure her I expected I had the "shivers" because everything in my life was so different now, and I didn't know what to expect. And I asked her then what did she think was going to happen around here?

Now, Mom's one of the most reassuring of people (well, really I haven't known very many). But on the scale of one to ten, I expect she'd stack up to about 7½. I may have that wrong because I don't know much about numbers yet. But sometimes I come up with a pretty good guess and I fool a lot of people!

Anyway, here started some more hugs. Oh **yum**! And Mom tried to reassure me that things were going to be great, and I sort of thought so too – from the way they had started.

Well. Being cozy, and loved, and letting down my defenses – before I knew it, I'd blabbed about how scared I'd been one night a long time ago, when I'd had this awesome dream about a big bear chasing me through some weeds. And how I ran and ran, and couldn't get anyplace! And how scared I'd been!

But Mom almost immediately came up with some reassuring words about lots of people being afraid of the unknown.

And then she said **she'd** been dreaming last night, and thought she'd dreamed me! And how tickled she'd been when she wakened and looked across the room, and saw me sitting right there! Wasn't that great? She didn't have to say that just to make me feel good.

I was feeling good, just being there in her arms.

But suddenly she put me down, went flying across the room, picked up a piece of brown wool blanket from this big, accumulated pile of stuff in a basket, came across the room – and made me a "designer cape" out of this great piece of hand-loomed wool from Scotland.

My cape didn't work too well, though, so she draped it at one shoulder and pinned it with a gold anteek pin. H-e-a-v-e-n-l-y!!

I was warm, loved, and had a **home at last**!

Then reassuring words began to spill out of her smiling mouth, a lot of which I didn't understand until I came to be more acquainted with how humans think. Words that said she'd get scared lots of times just thinking bad things were going to happen. She called it "getting ahead of herself and borrowing trouble."

Then Mom said that nearly always, when she'd get right down to something she called the nitty-gritty (weird!) they didn't happen at all! That we just had to do our best, have faith that we could work things out, and not be afraid of life all the time.

I understand **THAT** – I'm no dummy.

6

DISORGANATED!

Maybe that "morning person" stuff Mom has been talking about, makes some sense. I really don't know. It does seem that some of our best talks come then, maybe because Mom isn't afraid to let those busy things out of her head. She knows I'll understand.

But I have to admit one thing: sometimes I have no idea what Mom's talking about. Like this morning, when she said a really peculiar thing to me: "You know, Charlie, it seems to me that every time I look around, you're looking right at me!"

Well, what else? After all, I've got eyes, haven't I?

I think she could tell I was puzzled, so she tried to explain something about "wires connecting" my eyes . . . and knowing they can't move, and some more stuff.

Well, I didn't know what to think about that. Kind of hurts my head to think about wires in my eyes, for Heaven's sake. But I guess that's just the way things go when people try to **manufacture** bears and don't let nature take its course.

I was still trying to understand what Mom meant about wires and my eyes, when something called "Thanksgiving" came and Mom got almost frantic. It seems to me, after she talked to me one morning as she ran by to start cleaning windows and put things away in our room, that what she explained about **Thanksgiving** had pretty much already come my way. Like being thankful to pieces that I had a good home, and somebody to love me. Plus I was beginning to make the acquaintanceship of some pretty interesting friends in our room.

But Mom said to me that Thanksgiving is a one-day celebration. And that relatives were coming, and she didn't know how on earth she was going to get everything clean and orderly and fix all that food, and do something called "cope."

At least that's the word I think she used.

She also said Father wasn't the least bit perturbed, and kept telling her to slow down. And that **this** was the problem: she'd slowed down too much, and so had Father, and while she "loved those kids to pieces," she sure was going to have to put things up so they couldn't reach them. (I didn't know until later that "things" included me, and that she forgot to do that, what with this big rush and all. And that I'd rue the day Thanksgiving arrived!)

Well, some way, with Father pitching in, everything was in "apple-pie order" that morning. And I was just sitting there, listening to all the talk coming from the living room, and smelling the good smells floating all around, when these two, small, toddling female-persons came into my room. I couldn't tell one from the other, since they had on identical girl-stuff clothes. But one was bigger than the other, and after she looked at me (lovingly, I thought), she smiled and picked me up.

But here was this other smaller thing, and she evidently decided since she was smaller, **she** had rights too, and away I went from one to the other, now stuck under smaller person's arm – head down!

DISORGANATED! Didn't know what to think! Made a **very** undignified entrance into the midst of a charming, smiling bunch of big persons. Nobody seemed to be much disturbed, except I suddenly saw a stricken look on Mom's face, which she hid quickly, being the polite, loving person she is.

And then, Mom saved the day! Quietly she said: "Oh Kala! I have the dearest little bears, and I'll bet they would just love to go home with you and Kristin. They have some clothes, too (*not like Charlie!*), and a little suitcase, and we could pack them for your trip home."

"Charlie might have some germs (?!!) on him. He's pretty old," she added (*and about here things got <u>really</u> bad*) "and I need to dry-clean him before you handle him much!"

Whatever she meant, it sounded gruesome to me, but I thought I'd wait to discuss this 'til later, and thankfully found myself going back to our room, this time on a high shelf.

Well, the day went on **i.n.t.e.r.m.i.n.a.b.l.y.** (One of Mom's favorite words). I could hardly wait to have this discussion with her about this whole germ thing.

That night, when she came into our room, I said: "Have we got time now to talk about this germ/dry-cleaning stuff?"

But Mom answered quickly, "Charlie, sometimes Moms have to stretch the truth to save the day. My feet are killing me, Father's gone to bed and that's where I'm heading too!"

"I've been worrying about the condition of your body (***??!!***) and about getting some new clothes for you, but don't you worry – I'd never let anything **bad** happen to you, for you're a very special bear, and things are going to get better!"

Reassuring, that's my Mom!

7

FOREBEARS AREN'T FOUR BEARS

I've found it's not very hard for Mom to become obsessed. At least that's what she calls it, and I guess I kind of know generally what it means. She's mentioned it often enough.

First she got obsessed about my book – until I got her off the hook and took over myself. Now she's got obsessed talking about my clothes. How she knows I need something more appropriate to wear. Doesn't know what it should look like. Wonders if she could make it herself? Knows she has a lot of materials.

Boy! Is **that** an understatement! If you saw her linen/sewing/closet you'd think she could outfit every bear in the United States.

I figured she missed the point completely some time back, when I pointed out how furry Big Red bear was. And how maybe somewhere there might be some fur for me. And now she's begun to talk about something called "styles." Then I remembered one time I heard her say something like "clothes-don't-make-a-man" when she'd been talking to Father about a new pin-striped suit he'd bought. Which she said kind of reminded her of "gangsters," and I wondered what that had to do with **my** suit.

Anyway, this new obsession about my clothes went on for quite a while, but just as I thought I was about to finally have some real clothes and maybe some beautiful golden fur, here came a new obsession: something she called a search for her Scots "Fourbears!"

I don't understand. I know it's impossible, but it sounded to me like Mom meant she learned she had bears in her family!

One morning, when she was on my clothes-trail and she sat looking in my eyes, she came up with a statement about thinking I looked like a Stalwart Scots Chieftain . . . because of the steadfast expression on my face. And wouldn't it be great if we could outfit me in something she called a tar-tan suit?

"Isn't tar something sticky and dirty, Mom?" I asked, confused.

Mom just smiled and shook her head. "You're right, Charlie," she said. "But that's not what 'tartan' means," she said, showing me a framed photograph of Mom and Father surrounded by this plaid-type stuff, and two numbers.

"What are the numbers for," I asked, ashamed I still was having problems with numbers, even though I was doing my utmost best to understand those pesky things. "**5 0**, Charlie," Mom said. "This is a photograph of our 50th Wedding Anniversary. Father wanted it framed with my family's tartan pattern. Tartan is the name for special patterns of materials Scots people used to wear all the time to identify the family they came from."

"Tar-tan," I repeated once again, still confused.

She'd already mentioned this Scottish "thing" that wonderful first day when she wrapped me in a piece of her special Scotland wool and fashioned it with her anteek Scottish thistle pin. She smiled at me as if this explained it.

Well, I have to say I didn't understand the connection at all, but apparently that's the way her brain works sometimes.

Now, I am not going to tell you that things went along smoothly after that to get clothes for me. Mom talked out loud to herself a lot in the coming days, in between lots more things that were going on – like getting ready for another holiday . . . more relatives coming . . . going to visit somebody sick . . . trying to help Father figure out enough to do when he retired. Mom's discussions with me about all these things went on and on, and still no fur for me. No Scots tar-tan outfit either.

And though I mentioned a couple of times that maybe, maybe there might be golden fur to finish up the rest of me, it seemed to fall on deaf ears.

All these conversations between Mom and me naturally drifted into the other room, where Father was sitting, reading his financial papers, or cleaning out files. And a time or two he'd call out, asking if Mom was talking to him, and did she want an answer, dear?

And Mom, quickly realizing what she had done, would say "Oh no! I was just thinking out loud."

Meanwhile, I was on the other end of the conversation, just waiting for this one to resolve itself, wondering just how she was going to get out of it this time. But each time Father was satisfied, and went on with what he was doing. And Mom would wink at me, and I'd give her an understanding lift of an eyebrow to let her know I understood.

Once she told me something about Father I could hardly believe. "Do you realize, Charlie," she asked me, "Father has been working to earn a good living and support his family even longer than you were stuck in that dreadful box?"

Wow! Was I impressed! The whole time I'd been stuck in that box with poor Squirrely and that darned egg beater, becoming an almost-anteek in the process, Father was working hard, supporting his family, becoming an almost-anteek too! Mom said he started working to support his mother and baby sister when he was only a little boy, after almost all the rest of his family died during something terrible called the "Great Flu Epidemic."

So here he was, getting ready to re-tire, and Mom was worried he might not have enough interests, besides the cats, rescuing other animals, and working in the yard, to keep him occupied.

Now I appreciated all these things about Father, but I sure wished he'd talk to me some. Given all the important things he had done and seen in his life, I just knew he would have lots of things to teach me, and we could become best friends.

(Well, not exactly best friends. That's what Mom and I are. But we could become "almost best friends," that's for sure.)

I don't know what the thread of understanding is between teddy bears and humans, but evidently Father and I hadn't found it yet. But I loved him and figured things would work out between us in time, for he did talk to the cats a lot. But then, they've known each other for fifteen years, so maybe it would just take us time.

Well, "time" just seemed to get really misplaced about then. Mom said the holidays were almost here. I had lots of questions to ask her about, like what, exactly, were holidays? She didn't realize that, other than Sally's mother buying me as a birthday present, I had never seen any other kind of special days, because I was in a box. In an attic. So it didn't take long to understand this "holidays" thing was very important to people. I watched and listened, and waited for moments with Mom, so I could learn more about why "holidays" were so special.

Suddenly she would fly through the room, getting boxes of really interesting decorations down from the shelves. And magically a tree appeared in the living room! It smelled really good – just like being outside.

The cats evidently had just been waiting for the tree, and the shiny things Mom and Father put on it. And their sneaky paws would play with the lower ones, and then **crash**! There'd go another one. And Father agreed with Mom one morning that they'd just decorate outside next year. Let some poor, unsuspecting evergreen from the forest go on living . . . maybe buy one with something called burlap on it, and then set it out after Christmas. And a lot of sensible things like that.

So there really wasn't any time now to think about my clothes. Anyway, it didn't seem the monumental thing to me that it did to Mom. So I just used the time to get better acquainted with the other friends in my room. And believe me, there were a lot!

If I could have counted, I think I would have come up with something Mom calls an indeterminate number. Forty-six? But somehow that didn't seem to be nearly enough numbers. For they sat, and stood, not only on a blue shelf next to my chair, but they surrounded me on my chair, which was already really crowded. And they sat/stood/lay on what Mom called her "pride and joy," a pine, anteek "bride's chest" which went all along under our big front window.

"That's what a bride-to-be filled with her treasures years ago, Charlie, before she got married," Mom said one morning. "It's full of rugs I've woven for our girls, and anteek coverlets, and quilts . . ." (and about here she stopped and looked all around, I thought maybe counting friends' noses?)

So I said to her something about maybe some of "them" were living in there, and maybe we'd better look. But she replied quickly that she was almost sure they were all accounted for. Then, startled, said something (under her breath almost) about wondering – where had "Beaner" gone? She knew she could not have put him in the sack for needy children; he was "so dear to me – oldest daughter brought him all the way from California, and I would never give him away!"

She looked really happy then when she evidently spied him almost hidden behind "Grumby Bear," sitting on his chair with "Little" and "Mouse," and muttered something about trying to finish their story soon for little children. Evidently Mom forgot all about my original question about lifting the lid to see these "treasures for our girls." So I asked her again, but the phone rang about then, and I only half-heard her reply. But I thought she said something about . . . proper introductions . . . when she had more time.

I just looked around some more, and here was one I knew I surely couldn't have overlooked! Furry-all-over – a bear? Hard to tell though, for his ears (if he had any) were hidden by this black fox-trimmed hat, which I thought was pretty strange. Why hadn't I seen him before?

Well, about this time Mom came hurrying back, some emergency to go out on evidently. She began to re-attire herself quickly, telling me this emergency thing couldn't wait. Before she could escape again, I said to her I didn't remember seeing that "friend" in the hat. "How could I have overlooked him or her before, Mom?" I asked.

Mom's explanation sounded sort of odd, I thought, but from what I pieced together she'd been to another auction last night and it was late when she came in. "Buster" (evidently this furry thing) had most of the fur worn off around his ears. Mom said she had this expensive fox hat she'd had trouble explaining to Father – such a bargain! She hadn't found an appropriate time to wear it, though. "So," Mom said as she ran from the room, "the hat was too good to waste. Don't you agree he looks charming, Charlie?"

Well, I didn't know about "charming" exactly. But I figured it was none of my business, and went back to thinking about my lack of fur, when this "thing" had fallen heir to all this hair.

Was I glad Big Red was facing the other direction, and evidently hadn't noticed Buster yet, for I felt indubitably B.R. would be upset. Maybe even upset enough to try to help Mom understand why he thought this whole animal-fur-trapping-thing was so gruesome.

Just about then I gave up trying to pin names on any of Mom's other "friends," 'cause I wasn't going to try to solve the mystery of why Mom has accumulated so many. I'm not envious of any of them either – well, maybe I would like to have some more fur pretty soon. But you see, I know just where I stand with my Mom, and that's pretty reassuring for a half red-flannel/half-mohair, formerly abandoned, almost anteek teddy bear.

Compared to what happened the next morning, it all seemed pretty insignificant anyway, for I awoke to the sound of music.

I tell you, I **really** got the shivers!

From the radio, half-buried under a sliding stack of some of Mom's and my unfinished papers, came this SOOOOSA MARCH. I heard it years ago when Sally and I lived on the Army post! I'D HAVE KNOWN THAT SONG ANYWHERE!

Drums. And big brass horns! And marching feet. Marching to WAR!

And then the strangest thing ever happened: I hardly know how to tell you this. But suddenly a big, single tear splashed down on my old black foot! But it wasn't mine. It was Mom's! She was standing, looking down at me, and she picked me up and gave me the best hug yet. She could tell I had some tears too. But mine were inside, running into my stomach.

"Oh Charlie!" Mom said. "How many things you've taught me! We'll not dress **you** in an Army uniform, or any other dear little boy-child, either!"

You know, as ambiguous as that sounded, I sort of got it.

8

SOMETIMES TEDDY BEARS HAVE HORMONES TOO

Soon Christmas came and went, in a flurry of baking, eating, relatives, carolers outside the windows, tiny lights twinkling in the evergreens. Everything nice and cozy.

But I was sure glad I had taken over my book, for Mom wouldn't have had time for **that**!

Mom hung a little pair of red mittens on the tree for me, and me with nothing for her. It made me feel sad. I didn't know of anything I could give her – except a hug. And Mom said that was the best part of Christmas anyway. "Christmas," Mom told me, as I was still trying to understand more about special days that humans celebrated, "Christmas, Charlie, is about Love, and Peace, and Sharing." All kinds of good stuff like that.

"All the glitter and crowded malls, and people trying to outdo each other with gifts, is just x-traneous matter that doesn't mean a thing."

That's what Mom said.

"Christmas is for kids anyway." That's what Father said, while I was sitting in the living room on Mom's lap, enjoying the pretty lights on the tree, annoyed when one of the cats Father calls "Foosh" (even though her name is Seafoam), promptly hopped up on the couch and started sniffing me.

The other cat, named Goldie, was stretched out on Father's lap, purring while he rubbed her ears. "This year I do **not** want a bunch of things," Father continued. "I've got plenty. Just send money down to the child-aid department and to the animal shelter."

Mom said they went through this every year with Father, but he knew that their girls would buy him things anyway, because they loved him so much and wanted him to have packages to open.

Well, I didn't know what on earth I was going to do with those red mittens, but I did think, if I had a coat or something to go with them, it would be fun to wear them in the snow, which was coming down pretty good now. Maybe I could even learn to make a snowball and play with the kids congregating in the circle in front of our house. But I guess that wasn't appropriate, and nothing happened, so I just wore them on my paws, and dreamed that sometime I'd get to go with Mom on some of those "errands" she was always running out to do.

And then one morning she **did** invite me to go with her! Said she had a neat idea for trimming my proposed suit. Needed some braid; had to go to the Library and lots of places, and maybe we would even stop in at this "crafty place" where they sold **doll** clothes. (For Heaven's sake!)

Now I'd had about enough of that doll stuff forever, what with being stripped of my dignity, living in that pink-checked dress! But the trip sounded pretty exciting, and Mom could teach me lots more about the outside world, so we took off, me in my cape, Mom saying it looked appropriate for cold weather.

Here I thought I was going to try on some new clothes at this shop. But after she'd run the other errands, and time was running short,

Mom said something as she got out of the car. "I admit, Charlie, that I'm different, but I don't want to add to the public's opinion of me by traveling around with a teddy bear."

And so I just sat in the car and thought about that, and never could decide what she meant.

After a good while had gone by, and I'd been sitting there, watching cars coming and going, and people going into the shop, suddenly I heard this small-person voice coming from outside my window, and then I saw a little round head peering in at me. Then it made a little squeak and it said: "Oh, Mommy! Look at that cute bear! Can I take him home with me?"

!!! Well, even though I don't really know much about time, middle age is what Mom says I am. And cute? Oh well now! So I frowned and tried to look fierce, and I guess it worked to a degree, because the small-thing's older person took her by the hand and led her away.

But not before I'd had a glimpse of this dear little girl-bear in the squeaker's arms, outfitted in a blue coat and a bonnet with flowers on it. I turned my head and watched as they disappeared into their car, and I thought girl-bear maybe looked back at me!

Now, I don't understand about hormones. Mom mentions them every once in a while, but I haven't figured out how she uses the word or what it means. But something stirred, up in about the place where I guess humans' hearts are, and I felt happy and sad all at the same time. And a very strange feeling came over me, and I realized I was lonely – but I didn't know for what.

About this time Mom came out of the shop, got into our car, put a striped sack on the back seat, mentioned something about a "surprise," and didn't tell me what was in the sack. Wrapped me up a little better, and off we went for home. (Me thinking still of that little girl-bear.)

Back and forth Mom went at home, unloading groceries, and library books, and all the stuff she'd bought. And it was getting kind of dark about this time, and I wasn't too warm after she'd turned off the car. I figured she was putting away the groceries and stuff inside, and maybe getting supper started, so I just took a nap for a while.

Suddenly I heard Father pull in behind our car in the drive, and it was snowing pretty hard now, and it was dark! So I thought maybe he'd hear me if I called out to him, although I should have known better after all these months of non-communication.

So I called: "Yoo-Hoo, Father. Over here in Mom's car, Father."

But Father just walked up the driveway, and across the yard.

"YOO-HOO FATHER! It's me – it's Charlie! Mom's forgotten me in her car!"

Slight pause. Father turned around, looked, and then went on.

The back door closed. Is there something he'd forgotten? Will he come back? Will Mom ever realize she's left me out here to die in the cold by myself?

And I guess when Father mentioned to Mom that he thought maybe he'd heard a neighbor's child calling to him with a "yoo-hoo," she just about scorched the spaghetti sauce she was finishing for their supper. (At least that's what she told me when she put me on my chair in my nice warm room, after she'd run frantically out the back door, through the snow, and grabbed me.)

Funny thing, though. No apology for this **BIG ENORMOUS OVERSIGHT** of Charlie sitting in the car, freezing, forgotten. Mom said something to me about how she couldn't believe it! Thought Father was going to be opening up a line of communication with me soon.

Whatever that meant.

9

DETERMINATED

Up until now I hadn't paid much attention to how the weather affected humans. Bears too, I guess. After all, I couldn't see much all those years in the attic, so I really didn't know what time of year it was. Sometimes I just felt the cold as it crept in through the cracks, then that smothery heat when Squirrely and I would just about bake.

But now we had this winter-stuff, and mountains of snow. The difficulty of trying to overcome Nature and keep our feet on the ground (to quote Mom), began to affect us all.

One day she said something to the effect that even "intrepid" Father was going to have to give up driving clear to the city in this bad weather. Then Mom asked him, "Don't you think it's about time for you to retire and stay home and enjoy yourself?"

Finally something called a Retirement Dinner came along. I didn't know what that was, but Father didn't seem too happy when they came home. I figured the food hadn't been all that great.

But Mom said he was sort of depressed, because now he felt his main purpose in life was gone. He wouldn't see his associates and friends any more. One morning she said there were times he was beginning to act like a bear and growl!

But most of the time, Mom said, the growling would end in a big bear hug, and then he'd laugh and be cheerful for a while. I was happy when they began to go out on some trips and some shopping expeditions, and fill in the rest of the time getting used to each other again.

Well, I'd think fifty-plus years of being together should have made them used to each other by now, so I couldn't figure out what Mom was trying to explain.

But sometimes, when they'd come back from a trip, I'd hear Father explode about the traffic and the drivers. And Mom agreed and said she thought something she called a galoop was going to run right over their back bumper if they didn't get out of his way! I gathered from this that lots of cars were being driven by people who didn't have enough sense to drive.

And then I got sad when Mom said they'd about given up on a winter vacation trip they'd been dreaming about. She thought we all needed to take it easy for a while, get re-organized, think things over. That's about all I had to do anyway, so I didn't see anything much about it that was so different from what we already had. When Father and his systematic approach took over Mom's pantry one day, I understood what Mom was trying to explain.

She couldn't find anything now . . . where on earth has he put all my tools? Can't even find a nail to hang a painting. Lots of words like that, all in a restrained tone of voice. (Didn't want to discourage Father, you see.)

Well, nobody wanted to discourage Father. They just wanted him to be cheerful, and whistley, and happy like he used to be. So one day I thought I'd come up with something. I suggested to Mom they needed what humans call a change of scenery. I told her Big Red could help me take care of things around the house. If they couldn't take the big trip they had been planning, couldn't they at least get away for a few days?

"Well, maybe," Mom replied. But she'd have to investigate getting someone to feed the cats. And bring in the mail. And other "necessary evils" like that, Mom said.

But she came back home that morning looking pretty discouraged. Said she'd been turned down when she talked to a couple of people.

I felt sad for Mom, 'cause I thought the vacation was a good idea, and I could tell she was looking forward to Father and her going someplace.

"I haven't given up on us taking a trip for a few days, Charlie," she said finally, with a determinated expression. "I just need a few minutes to rebuild my positive juices with some hot T. I'll contact a couple of other friends. I'm sure one of them will come to our rescue."

While we were talking in what Mom calls a "positive vein," I decided I'd slip in a positive mention about the still-not-done suit, or new fur for Charlie. Although, all things considered, I was pretty content, because my life was so good compared to what I'd had.

I also knew how lucky I was not to have to have any "major surgery" like poor Squirrely was still having done at The Doll Lady's. 'Cause his tail was so stuck together from all that candlewax melting when we were in the cardboard box, even Mom couldn't get him all cleaned up. Mom told me her friend had to do something awful called amputate Squirrely's tail, and was making him a new one.

So I told Mom, much as I wanted to look more appropriate, I knew getting Squirrely well was more important than new clothes for me. Mom had already proved how much she loved me, and I was warm and cozy in my wonderful new home, and among new friends, so she sure didn't have to worry about this suit.

I don't know why on earth she hadn't thought of it, but suddenly I had this big, momentous idea. Goodness knows, Mom's talked a lot of times about this weaver/knitter/friend of hers. Even has a beautiful sweater the friend knit for her. "Friend" lives a few miles away and raises sheeps. Now I'm not familiar with sheeps, but I think they grow wool. So I figured my mohair fur maybe had originally come from something like sheeps.

A lot of planning, talk-planning, temporary stuff had gone on about my suit all these weeks, but when I asked Mom, she still looked sort of vague about sheeps sharing some wool. Then she went on cleaning out a drawer or something. She did say she'd think about this; maybe she'd give Barbara (the friend) a ring. Pretty soon now, she said.

And that was the end of that.

No call to Barbara, no more mention. The whole idea just fell down in a hole, with a lot of other things.

Well, I'm a bear who likes to get to the end of things, for goodness sakes! It didn't seem like any big deal to me, to call this friend and get those wheels rolling. So I did. Early one morning, when nobody was up but me and the cats, I called.

Barbara-friend sounded so nice when she answered the phone, said "I'll be so glad to see you all. Maybe I do have some furwool for this bear Charlie."

(OH BOY!)

"We're having a lot of lambs dropping right now," she added. (Sounded intriguing. I wondered what on earth she meant?) She thought they might have to run to the barn. (She and Stephen: her husband, I guess, me not having met either one of them.) "Come right on out," she said, "but be sure to call first."

Poor Mom. When I relayed the message, she was about as taken aback as I've ever seen her. Said she would have to do something she called cover her tracks. "Oh dear," she told me. "Maybe I can pretend it's that darned answering-machine I can't work. Voices sound funny on it. I'll really have to think about how I'm going to get out of this one! Wherever did you learn to do that, Charlie?" More stuff like that.

Shoot! It taught me one big thing: there's hardly anything you can't conquer if you put your mind to it. You just have to get up off your chair, put one foot in front of the other, think positive – and do it!

10

TRUE LOVE CAN MAKE YOU GROW ABOUT A FOOT

Even though I had hoped we could go see the sheeps and get some furwool, nothing happened right away. Things went along on pretty much an even keel for a while, what with all this snow-stuff outside, and everybody being afraid to get out on the ice. So Mom, Father, and the cats and I were all really cozy and sort of shut in, in our own little world. (Me still writing away on my book.)

But one morning Mom said something really unexpected to me about being just about ready to give up! I didn't know whether she meant my fascinating life story or hers. She thought maybe the things we'd been trying to write about weren't very important. Maybe there wasn't enough adventure or sex, and things we wrote about were just "ordinary, every-day living stuff," she said.

Well, I don't know much about "sex." I knew there was an awful lot of talk about it on the TV, and some of it seemed pretty far-out to me. And I figured sex had something to do with people mating for life. (But then most bears do that, too.) But I was learning that people don't seem to be satisfied with just one mate anymore, so their kids get all messed up with "steps" and "step/grands" and "half-siblings" and "your kids," and "my kids" and all that unsettling stuff.

I tried to be reassuring as I conversed with Mom, telling her that what we had sounded pretty good to me. I thought maybe there was a large segment of the population who'd really appreciate us getting down to the basics. After all, I might not know everything, but I sure knew our lives were more interesting than most.

A few days later Mom discovered this piece of material she called tar-tan in her closet, and it seemed she could better focus on our project now that she'd found it. She began to describe this Scots / Chieftain / Clan thing again. She told me how brave the men of Scotland had been, fighting to defend their homeland. And how this stuff called tar-tan was their badge of courage! Well, this piece of tar-tan didn't look all that fantastic to me. I'd have to say it looked sort of faded, but Mom called it the ancient version of the pattern for the "Clan of the MacDonalds," which her great-grandmother brought to North Carolina when they moved here from Scotland. But somehow, that piece got lost. Just a few years ago Mom discovered the exact same thing in this catalog that put out things made for people with something she called ties to Scotland.

"Is that why Father doesn't wear those ties you got him, since he came from someplace else called Po-land?" I wanted to know.

Mom just smiled, kind of distracted-like. She gets that way sometimes.

I let the subject drop, still not certain why the word "ties" apparently meant different things. This language stuff can sure be confusing.

About this time I asked her why America was supposed to be something called a melting pot, 'cause I wasn't sure just what that meant. I don't even know where I heard it. And Mom looked at me, startled, like I'd said something important!

She thought a minute then said she wondered if people hadn't melted together quite enough, and wondered if all these ethnic groups who were always fighting couldn't better spend their time trying to find their likenesses, instead of their differences.

Well shoot! Just when I thought things were getting really interesting, she made a dash for the other room to finish something else.

Later that day, when supper was over and Father was at a Humane-Dog-Type-Organization and things were quiet for a little while, Mom said she'd put off the suit long enough! Sure enough, here she came with a tape-measure-thing, the piece of tar-tan, and a lot of big ideas.

Oh my!

Mom began to measure me, first one way and then the other, and that was really hairy! For somehow, the figures didn't please her. "They just aren't anything like I thought they'd be, Charlie," she said.

I didn't know why. I thought I was just a plain, up-and-down teddy bear, with a few curves and that old red flannel.

So I sort of wished I hadn't brought this to her attention in the first place. Right about then I sort of began to understand what Mom had meant about being a day-dreamer. I don't believe she sees things quite like other people. Maybe she's even trying to do the expedient thing, like using this tar-tan material which equals Scotland to her?? Overlooking completely the fact that I'm just a fifteen-inch semi-anteek teddy that other people wouldn't see very much remarkable about.

But when my Mom looks at me with those soft crinkles around her eyes, I guess I can sort of daydream too. She said to me one time that True Love can make you grow about a foot, and I believe that's got something to do with it!

11

WUNZ AND TREWS AND OTHER HIGHLY IMPORTANT NUMBERS

By now I think Mom and I both realized, if anything was ever going to be done, we were going to have to do something about my suit. So why weren't we going out to this Barbara-person's and begging for some sheep wool?

But I knew icy roads and all made Mom apprehensive, plus she was not too keen about turning Father loose on the l-o-n-g River Hill. She didn't mention anything about the galoops, though, so I figured maybe they hibernated in the winter.

Sure enough, Mom decided we should wait some more. "Just a little while longer, Charlie," she said.

Just about then Mom said she'd had a really great idea! Oh no, I thought. Not again! "The Doll Lady, who is helping fix poor Squirrely, and who created Big Red, sews all kinds of things. I'll just bet she could make this tar-tan suit!" Evidently something's getting started, for she called her and made an appointment for the very next day to go see about my suit!

Later that same day Big Red told me that he sure would like to watch the I.U. basketball game on the TV, but he hardly ever got invited to go in the living room and watch. (Too quiet. That's what

I think about him.) But him being such a loyal I.U. fan and all, I thought it worth a mention, and when I told Mom, she went right along with the idea. We all congregated in the living room, Father in his easy chair, half-watching, half-reading.

Mom has some really neat books with stuff about Scotland, and we were all sitting there, Big Red, eyes looking intently at every play; father doing something he calls "listening with one ear." (Strange! I wonder how he does that?) Meanwhile, I was perched on the back of the couch, so I could look over Mom's shoulder at the books. We were all cozy as could be, Mom happily singing to herself, quiet-like, something about Bluebells of Scotland.

Then she turned a page – and here were all those stern-looking Scots-persons, in every kind of outfit – but – GET THIS! They had on pleated skirts!

Well, I about fell off the couch. I decided this was the reason Mom hadn't been all that explicit when we'd talked about the style of my new suit. Not something with a yukky, sissy skirt, for gosh sakes!

But Mom grabbed me and pulled me down on her lap just as the phone rang at halftime. Father left to answer it. Then Father, who was really worked up about the coach's bad words, said words that Mom told me is "expletive stuff." When we started to write, Mom had warned me "not to use any of these, Charlie." To tell you the truth, I didn't care because I was still in a state of shock, just thinking about this unspeakable thing I thought Mom had in mind for my suit!

But after Father left, she began to reassure me that she hadn't set her mind about the style and promised me we'd find something appropriate. And when she turned the page – there it was!

This really handsome Scottish hunk, with a tar-tan cap of some kind, a jacket Mom said was velvet, and neat looking pants with a crease in 'em. Just like I'd had so many years before with my army uniform! Only they seemed to be cut a little different, or maybe it was the way he wore this sash-thing over one shoulder, and some kind of a pouchy pocketbook thing hanging down in front, with fur around the edge.

I said I sure didn't need that; I didn't have any money or keys. Mom said not to worry about that. It was something she called x-traneous anyway.

There were some more alphabet letters underneath the picture, and I asked her to spell this for me, since I'm trying to broaden my mind and learn a few things which seem really important.

"T-r-e-w-s," Mom said. "'Trews' is Scots dialect for trousers."

Well nuts! I thought sure I had that word pinned down some days before, when she'd been trying to help me with numbers.

"Truze?" I said. "Now correct me if I'm wrong, but you said that truze comes after wunz. Is there some kind of a secret code thing when it comes to clothes, so the jacket is the wunz, and the pants are the truze?"

Mom just smiled, and pretty soon she, Big Red and me went off to bed too. (Or is it "I" went off to bed? Anyway, we did! Went off to bed, that is.)

But Mom wrote a pome for me before she went to sleep, then said, "this will explain things, Charlie." But it didn't. Explain things, that is.

I'll share it, though, and maybe you, being a human being, you'll get it.

WORDS! WORDS! WORDS!

Roots/routes   Right/write   Ones/Wunz   Twos/Trews

There are some things in the World of Man
*Which do not **bear** explaining.*
By the time you figure out the words
You'll just end up complaining
That the whole thing's foolish anyway,
For there is no one "right" way
To solve the problems facing us
When we get up every day!

*So grin and **bear** it, Charlie Bear*
I'll try to do the same
For life is full of wunz and trews
And words which sound the same.

12

JAMMY TRAUMAS

While Mom and Father were busy with other things, I spent the next few days doing something my Mom calls "pondering the imponderables." Thinking about the Scottish hunk, about the sheeps, and about the surprise Mom told me she had for me when I went with her a few days ago. I supposed my surprise was in the striped sack she'd put on the back seat of the car.

I casually mentioned to her that I couldn't ever remember having a surprise in my whole life, and I surely hoped it wasn't like the surprise I had that day when I ended up in a box, forgotten in grandmother's attic until Mom rescued me.

Mom looked surprised and wondered what she'd done with her sack? While she looked all around our room, I gently reminded her that the last time I'd seen it, it had been on the back seat of our car. "Maybe," I said, "maybe, Mom, it's still there."

She didn't seem convinced. But after looking everywhere – in the closets, under stacks of magazines and our writings – Mom finally took my suggestion and went out to the car. Sure enough! The sack was in the car. So here she came, "lost sack" in her hands.

But I could see, for some reason, Mom seemed nervous about opening the sack, and began to tell me that this was just a temporary "stop-gap" measure. Finally, she opened the sack and pulled out this blue-and-white striped suit with a jacket and pearl buttons and pants! I didn't mention that it looked like maybe it was for a Doll! I could see she was already nervous, and I sure didn't want to add to her trauma. (She's got several of those already.)

And now, at last, that pink dress came off!

But during all that time, was she looking at my new suit or the old pink girl's dress? No! She was just standing there, looking pretty startled. Then, when I looked down, so was I! For I had not realized until that very minute, that not only did I have black feet — I had NO KNEES! Just straight, unbending black legs and feet.

No wonder I hadn't been able to sit down, and had stood there . . . like a "Stalwart Scots Chieftain." I didn't have any choice!

Well, Mom pulled herself together before I did, and began to talk in a practical way about "pants just a mite too long; I'll hem them up as soon as I can."

Then her voice sort of trailed off, and I could see she was thinking seriously about something. Far-away look. Since I've begun to know her better, I figured something pretty ponderous was going to come out of her mouth any time now. And it did.

"You were right about that crummy manufacturer, Charlie!" She picked me up and sat down on the chair, and looked into my eyes. "You're truly unique. I don't know of any other teddies made just like you! I guess you'd be happier if you'd been furry-all-over, and had joints, but there are millions of bears like that. It's your differences that make you unique."

Well, I sat there, all warm, and loved, thinking about all that "unique" stuff, and I thought back to the long-ago time when I'd stood on a toy-shop shelf. It seemed to me I remembered several of "us" who'd been made exactly the same. But having been fifty-plus years, I sort of thought my shelf-mates had long since either been loved to pieces, or some collector-person had grabbed them.

So I knew just how lucky I was to have someone who loved and appreciated me just for what I am!

A 15" semi-anteek teddy with old red flannel, no knees, and black legs and feet. And I loved my Mom even more for making me feel so special.

—⚏—

Well, I thought that was the end of that, and Mom would now hurry away to something more important or worthwhile. But evidently her gears weren't going yet, for she sat there with me hugged against her. I just stayed quiet, content and warm, pondering Life.

As I've thought about some of our problems and tried to help solve what I can, it occurs to me that these long conferences between Mom and me use up a good deal of time. Maybe time she should be putting to more constructive use. But she thinks some pretty worthwhile stuff gets solved once in a while, so I'm not gonna mention this to her.

Then Mom began to laugh, and said something to me about "that goofy idea you had about polka-dotted people, Charlie!"

Mom and I discuss so many things in our talks, I couldn't remember what she meant right away, but then I remembered it had to do with people's colors, and people being afraid when they meet someone who looks different from what they expect.

Mom reminded me I'd talked about polka-dots taking the place of the usual black or brown or yellow, or white-all-over people. So maybe, if I was polka-dotted instead of old red flannel, people might think

I was a clown-bear, and laugh happy-like, instead of laughing at me because I wasn't made like a "normal" teddy.

But this conversation had ended with a great big hug (yum!) from Mom, and her reassurance once more that "colors are such a tricky thing, Charlie. My painting colors are one thing, but colors of people are something else altogether."

Well, colors, differences, peoples — they all sort of floated around in my head when Mom suddenly ran to turn off the oven. And, as I sat there, I got almost aggravated!

Not because she'd mentioned my dream again about being chased by the big, big bear, and comparing it to fear people felt when faced with the unknown — but aggravated because I could see that Mom knew this color-stuff was something really important about life — and I couldn't connect it!

That evening, as I stood there in my striped doll suit, feeling really glad that maybe I looked a little more appropriate, even if it did gap at the neck and show my red flannel; and, even though my pants were a little too long, and I felt fairly sure Mom would never get around to hemming it up; anyway, still I felt pretty happy about the day's outcome.

Then I looked over at Big Red and, besides his embroidered-on-smile, I thought I heard a kind of snicker. (Did he know it was a doll's jammy suit? Did he think I didn't look appropriate?) But when I asked him, he mumbled something about how all that fur in his nose made him laugh sometimes. But then he snickered again, and I thought his smile got wider!

I've concluded one important fact from today's discussion: we can't dwell on our own problems all the time. We just have to realize that there are probably a lot of bears out there who are worse off than we are!

13

HUMANS HIBERNATE TOO

Right here I'm giving Mom credit: she did follow through with our appointment with the Doll Lady, and it all just went clickity-click! Which surprised me, as my suit project so far hadn't gone anywhere. But "Doll Lady is an expert," Mom had said.

Now Mom was pretty insistent that she didn't want my suit to end up looking like an Army uniform. Then, she and Doll Lady got into a long discussion about war, and me – having been so devastated when my Sally's father had marched off to that War-stuff – didn't want to listen. So I sort of took a slight nap, eyes open, ears not too alert.

I came to in a hurry, though, when I heard one of Mom's sentences end, saying something about like "Maybe it will look too dressy using velvet for the jacket?" (Am I ending up with another dress?) But I could see the pattern laid out on the tar-tan, and I thought it looked more like tailored pants.

They kept talking about some unpronounceable name of a General leading our boys through the expletive of this scorching desert war. Mom then saying something about a picture she thought she'd seen of a general with a teddy bear, who'd been a mascot for the troops? But then, maybe she'd dreamed that. She couldn't find the article, and said, "Don't quote me on that."

I guess Doll Lady knows Mom pretty well, 'cause she just smiled.

Anyhow, while they went on talking about this war stuff, and I sat there thinking about these heroes and generals and teddy bear mascots, I decided that maybe humans weren't much smarter than **I** was. Because, from what Mom and Doll Lady talked about, this war-stuff had been going on back through time. "And whole brave generations of boys marched off to defend some shining ideal which seemed then to be worth laying down their lives for," Mom said. And, how pitiful it was that lives were shattered in this devastation of War!

Well! Where on earth did Big Red get his "descoration" word I'd heard him use a couple of times? I know he's been to school! But in time-stuff he's younger than me so, evidently, me being boxed up in that attic, I've missed out on a lot of important things.

However, I can see that Mom isn't going to have much time to help me learn, for now a lot of her time's taken up with trying to find things for Father to do. Outside interests, she called it. And, as we drove home, instead of being relieved about my suit finally starting to be made, she was worrying about **this**.

So I said, "well, I don't think anybody can do much outside right now, with this cold and snow."

Then Mom said something that really confused me. She said "outside interests" didn't mean you were doing things outside!

Just as we arrived home, I remembered that awful "dressy" word, and I turned around and asked her about my suit. "Isn't it going to have a jacket and pants?"

"Oh, yes!" Mom said. (And it seems "dressy" is just another expression also and doesn't have anything to do with a dress!)

I gave up and just looked out the car window while I pondered how anybody **ever** learns to speak English!

Now Mom's always talking about stuff being appropriate, and I decided maybe my tar-tan suit would fall in that category if outside stuff was coming pretty soon. Like gardens? So, thinking I'd understood this one thing, I said to Mom how glad we all would be to get outside, but didn't she think overalls for me (and maybe Big Red) would be more appropriate?

I saw immediately that wasn't the thing to say, for Mom said overalls are just an impossible thing to sew for a bear! "For you don't have much waist to keep them up, Charlie, so we'd have to make a bib to make them, and I just don't believe I'm going to have time to worry about that!"

(Well, I'm sure not going to mention that again! Isn't a bib something for a baby? I wonder which is worse: a baby-bib or a dressy uniform which isn't a dress?)

About this time we arrived home, and as she took me to my room, I said something to her again about going to her friend's to see about my wool, thinking that the golden furwool suit would solve this whole thing. But Mom replied absently about icy roads. "But pretty soon, Charlie, surely it is going to be Spring. Then we'll see."

And with that I went back to my chair. I really didn't want Big Red to know how mixed-up I was about all those words. I did fill him in on our trip, but he didn't seem interested. Started talking about it being almost the end of basketball season at I.U. And he didn't think anybody was ever going to take him! Then he said he believed this sports-thing was getting out of hand. "Maybe I'm gonna think about 'vironmental things more. Maybe I could write a letter to Greenpeace and let them know I appreciate their efforts on behalf of all living things."

He said some other stuff I didn't understand, but which sounded pretty learned to me, and I wondered again where on earth he got his information?

All of a sudden-like, it seemed to me almost overnight – that cold winter weather just picked up and went away! The snow began to melt, and little green things Mom called shoots began poking their heads through the ground. Father began to whistle, and ran to the basement to bring up tools, and talked about uncovering stuff.

But Mom thought he was rushing the season. Father said he didn't know, but felt he'd x-pire if he didn't get out and put things write! (Or maybe that's "right?") I have got to impress on my Mom soon I need help with some of this important writing stuff.

About the time the little shoots peeked their heads out of the ground, the whole atmosphere in our house changed. I decided the gloomy feelings that seemed to descend on humans really **did** have something to do with the weather. I mentioned this again to Mom, and reminded her about hibernating, and asked her what was the difference between retiring and hibernating?

But she still maintained they were not the same. You sure could have fooled me! I can't see the difference.

As I sat there with my friends that night, thinking about the day's events, I felt glad that Father had come out of his den and was happily scratching around, uncovering stuff in the garden. Then I thought about bears uncovering their winter's cache that they store before they hibernate. And I sort of chuckled to myself, because I figured for once Mom was wrong: It seemed to me there were lots more similarities than differences between humans and my family!

So I felt pretty good that night, for though I knew I was mixed up about a lot of words, and I knew I wasn't appropriately dressed yet, I knew I was a pretty insignificant part of all the big things that fill this complicated world I'd suddenly found myself in. The main thing I knew was that I'd been one lucky teddy bear to have been rescued by my Mom!

14

SHEEPS!

My brain must have been wool-gathering, for suddenly one morning we were packing, and it seemed we were going to The Sheep Farm at last!

Even Father seemed excited, and he suggested a picnic, if the weather didn't decide to change again. He even said he'd pack the hamper while Mom finalized the details of our visit with Barbara and her husband.

I asked Mom was my new striped-suit appropriate to wear? She said maybe I'd better wear my cape too, and draped it a little better, re-pinning it with that thistley pin, "Courtesy of a long-ago Scots ancestor," she repeated once more, just in case I had forgot, which of course, I had not.

I really hoped she wasn't going to start on that ancestor stuff again. In fact, she seemed too busy right then. Suddenly she said she wondered if that tiny cemetery up on the hill near Barbara and Stephen's might have some of her relatives buried there. I reminded Mom we were supposed to see about my furwool and have a picnic, not look for ancestors.

Mom just smiled.

I learned something else before we went. Big Red is evidently smarter than I've been giving him credit for (but I do try to be fair about that). When we invited him to go too, I thought he turned down the invitation at first because he's so shy. But he began this long dissertation about not knowing if he could stand to ride through some **descorated** (here went that word again!) woodlands that had probably been descorated by non-environmental dopes who'd dumped old cars and 'frigerators and plastic stuff in there. Then, he said, little annymals would get that stuff in their craws! And a whole lot of other things which really got to me, because I decided indubitably that he could read!

But B.R. said "No." He could listen better, he said, because his ears are bigger than mine. That's for sure! Plus he's about three times my size, but his ears seem to be appropriate for the size of his other parts! (Except his legs are stubby.) Anyways, he said he overheard a lot of things when the radio or TV was on, and he heard Mom and Father talking a lot about important environmental things.

About then B.R. said he had changed his mind, because he was pretty bored and believed he would go after all.

After what B.R. told me, I decided I'd listen harder too; maybe I could pick up some **big** important stuff also.

There was lots of information and talk for me to listen to, all the way to The Sheep Farm, for Mom and Father chattered away like kids. And Father, who was driving, told Mom to "watch out for a certain tree."

"There it is!" he said suddenly, excited. The tree was where he and someone named Frank sat and had a picnic one day years ago, when they'd been duck hunting on the river.

Mom said she was sure he was right, given his remarkable memory. Well, I couldn't see anything so remarkable about that tree, but since it gave them pleasure, I felt good too. I love to see Mom and Father happy. Lots more reminiscences went on between them as they'd see other familiar spots. Then, as we rounded a sharp curve and started up a long, windy hill Mom suddenly exclaimed that she saw the cemetery where she wanted to look at the stones, if we could before we went home.

Just as Father started to say something . . . **I HEARD IT!**

Baä, baä, baäing of sheeps!

"**Sheeps, Mom, Sheeps!**" I exclaimed to Mom, forgetting that Father was in the car.

"Did you just say something?" Father asked Mom, swerving the car, startled.

Mom, recovering something she calls her composure, said she was talking to herself. Father gave her a strange look, then looked at the road ahead.

I couldn't stop staring out the window. I could tell they were sheeps. Looked just about right from what I'd seen in a couple of books. And they were all under a great big maple tree standing around looking real peaceful. And little baby sheeps were jumping around on funny, stiff-looking legs, and some of them were lying down, just looking friendly and chewing something.

But my heart sank! **WHERE WAS MY WOOL? MY BEAUTIFUL GOLDEN YELLOW WOOL**, like my head and paws?

This stuff they were wearing sure didn't look like anything I'd want to put on my body. It was sort of a dirty tannish grey, like the sheeps hadn't had a bath in a long time, and some of them had straw sticking to their furs, and altogether unsatisfactory stuff like that. And I'll tell you, **THE BOTTOM ABOUT FELL OUT OF MY HEART!**

But Mom, using this ESP which we have, glanced around quickly at me, and whispered something like, "They haven't been sheared yet, Charlie. The finished product isn't anything like what you see now. Those March winds would freeze the little newborn lambs, and my friends are waiting to shear the old wool, so that the mother ewes can protect the little lambs with the warmth of their bodies."

"**YOU'S**???"

I wonder if that's the word Mom meant to say? Do you suppose Mom has trouble with **Her** spelling too?

15

FURWOOL FOR CHARLIE

I've never seen Mom happier than she was as we began to unpack and get ourselves into a visiting mode!

This dear-looking female-person came down off the porch, across the drive. She and Mom had several big hugs and told each other how tickled they were to see each other. Father, having parked the car, got a big hug too, which I thought he looked embarrassed about, him evidently not being the really close friend that Mom and Barbara had become while they'd been weaving together.

Suddenly here came these two enormous animals, great big dogs, jumping and hopping around, what with being so happy to see someone they could jump on, and that suited Father just fine for, from what I can gather, he's just about an "animal-freak." At least, that's what Mom's called it more than once, when another animal comes across our back porch and he sees it's all forlorn and needs a home.

When that happens he tells Mom "We won't keep it long – just til we put an ad in the papers." Then, Mom says, he screens the applicants, just to be sure they're the right kind of person to have this animal. And sometimes they don't turn out to be, and this animal more or less takes up permanent residence, until an appropriate person can be found. Anyway, Father was happy as a lark, and after Barbara said her husband Stephen was up mending fences while the weather was nice, he decided he'd walk up through the meadow, then admitted maybe he'd sit down on the big stump halfway up the hill . . . legs aren't quite as dependable as they used to be. (Well, I sure know about **legs**. No knees. Just legs!)

So, off we went in different directions, B.R deciding to stay in the car and rest, me being lovingly held against Mom's shoulder (oh yum)! Father laughing, the dogs circling, X-static to have found someone who appreciated what they were trying to say!

Up the steps, into this really nice, warm house. Tall, enormous windows, sparkley sun shining through. Big, funny looking things sitting around with lots of threads on them, and pedals like a car has, and a funny round wheel-of-a-thing on spindly legs with more threads running around it.

About this time Barbara looked at me, gave me a little pat on my handsome golden head, then looked at Mom and said, "Is this your young friend you were worrying so about bringing out?"

Before Mom could answer Barbara looked at me and said: "What's your name, bear?"

Mom, being the self-possessed person she can be sometimes, quickly replied, "This is Charlie, Barbara, and I guess he's just about speechless! He's never been on a sheep farm before. In fact we don't know what his life was before he moved in with us!"

(Speechless!) Well, she didn't give me a chance to say anything, did she? And "moved in?" Who carried **who** out of that cold car that snowy sales day?)

Convoluted. That's Mom sometimes.

Well, she was smart enough not to mention anything about my telephone conversation. But Barbara, evidently having this well organized have-to-put-everything-in-proper-order mind, told Mom she thought she hadn't sounded quite herself that other morning, then decided it was because Mom had pried herself out of bed so early.

Mom looked right into her eyes and said, "If you only knew!"

It got even better as we went from room to room, and I could see they were so happy visiting, but I kept wondering when somebody was going to get around to mentioning anything about my wool stuff? Then we went into another room, and here were baskets, and more baskets, and a rack-thing hung with big, long bunches of what had a great similarity to the color I'd been searching for to make my suit!

Barbara, sizing things up in a hurry, and glancing from me to this one basket, exclaimed something like, "I figured that goldenrod dye of mine would achieve Charlie's beautiful color!" But I still couldn't see how we were to achieve something appropriate from these long strings of stuff. I figured though, she surely knew what she was talking about, for I saw these gorgeous rug-things coming off these "looms," and at this point, all I wanted to do was sit on that cozy-looking seat under the window and watch the sheeps.

And think about things, for it was turning out to be a pretty important day for me, and I needed to get things in what Mom calls their proper perspective.

As we went around a corner into another room, Barbara turned and said to Mom: "I forgot to tell you that we have a very special visitor. Uncle Ben, this is my weaving-friend and her friend, Charlie Bear." (Well, she might have given me more of a positive descriptive touch, something like . . . "this charming, heart-warming teddy, who's gracing their family with his presence" . . . or something.)

But I didn't want to appear rude, or conceited, 'cause I really wasn't, so I just looked at this dear little grey-ish man sitting in this great big chair. And such a kind smile came over his wrinkled face, all crinkley with that kind of look Mom gets when she's happy about something, and his arms reached out to me.

Well, I was sort of startled; this hadn't been in my scenario. But Mom said a few words to him about me needing some wool, and I wondered why she needed to call attention to that so early in our acquaintanceship.

But I was immediately distracted by the beautiful sounds which started coming from his smiling mouth. How they sounded!! Where had I heard them before?

Mom seemed startled too, and looked at Barbara with a question in her eyes. Barbara said Uncle Ben had been an archeologist all his life, and that he'd had something she called a stroke on his last "dig." (Did that have something to do with gardens? I couldn't wait to ask my Mom.) She told us he traveled all over the world pursuing "dreams of civilization long buried," and stuff like that.

So I figured maybe the sounds were something he'd dug up? I didn't know exactly. But I did know they filled someplace inside me that made me warm and happy!

"Even ancient languages are no problem for Uncle," Barbara continued. "But he speaks so many and shifts from one to another, that sometimes it's hard to follow him." Uncle Ben didn't seem perturbed at him having a mouth-piece, since he loved his niece and her husband. I could tell. And he went on with some beautiful, singing sounds, which seemed to fill the room and my heart with pure joy!

Since I could see he was a friendly type, I decided I would just cuddle down beside him while Mom and Barbara went into the other room to get on with something Mom told me several times before is "girl talk." I believe that age counting syndrome's sort of got mixed up in Mom's mind, although I've heard her say she made straight As in Math, and I think that's numbers. But "girl?"

So Uncle Ben and I kind of took a nap. While I was half dreaming, I thought I heard more of those beautiful sounds! And things were so peaceful and nice, I nearly went clear over the edge.

But all of a sudden, I woke up and heard this big conversation floating from the next room. Mom was telling Stephen about me needing some more fur . . . and on and on. Well, I'd never even met this Stephen-person. Did she need to tell him my innermost secrets?

Then I heard Stephen begin to reminisce about a bear he had when he was little. "I haven't thought of him in years." (Bad, bad!) "I wonder what happened to him?" (Now you wonder! I can tell you're no kid. Where've you been all those years?)

After Stephen admitted he thought his bear used to talk to him at night when his folks went downstairs and he was afraid and lonely, Mom said the most perceptive thing:

"UNIVERSAL JOY TO BELONG TO A TEDDY BEAR!!!!!"

NOW she's getting it right.

16

TO EVERY THING THERE IS A SEASON

Well, Mom had no more than uttered this erudite (that's what she calls it) statement, than suddenly all expletive busted loose! (See, you didn't think I knew what that meant, did you?)

Really strange, loud noises began to come from the barn behind the house, and I could hear part of what they were saying. "Oh, Great! I just knew those lambs would begin to appear the moment it got cold and snowed again!"

That was Stephen talking.

Then Barbara asked Mom if she'd mind checking things in the house while they went out to help someone named Heather. "She's planned triplets for us, and this is her first drop (??), so we may be out there a while. I'm afraid we'll have to cut our visit short."

Even Father got upset with the weather. "I cannot believe it's beginning to snow again," he said.

Only my Mom didn't seem the least surprised about the snow. According to her, lambs always get borned when the weather gets the worst. "At least that's the way it always was on the farm where I grew up," she said.

Much as I love to listen to Mom's long stories about her childhood, this was not the time, since everyone was in a hurry to go to the barn.

Mom came in and took me from Uncle Ben's arms and turned to

introduce Father to him. Then Father surprised both Mom and me, for he said something to Uncle Ben, who looked so happy he began to answer Father in those same-sounding words!

When Mom asked him to translate for us, Father told us he was pretty rusty, having not used his French since college days. Then he said, "I just had a feeling I could communicate with Uncle Ben, because I remembered some of the major digs used to be financed by The French Government!"

Well, I was so proud of Father. But I wondered why Father wasn't able to communicate with me? Was I gonna have to learn this "French stuff" so we could communicate when I'm still having such a hard time with just plain English?

Mom went into the nice warm kitchen to check the stove, and Father began to clear what Mom called the "elevenses T things." I didn't know what that was, but if I could have counted, I don't think I would have come up with that many "T"s.

Uncle Ben seemed to be cozy and warm, and my folks got everything else in order, so we took our picnic hamper and headed for the door, but Father insisted on going out first, to get our car started and warm before he would let us come out in the cold March wind.

Thoughtful. That's Father. Always.

17

LAMBS ARE LAMBS BUT SHEEPS AREN'T SHEEPS

While Father went to start the car, I decided to ask Mom to help me understand a couple things which I'd worried about almost since we came. I asked Mom if Uncle Ben's stroke had made a kind of fur in his mouth, like mine. And was that the reason things sounded so different when the sounds came out?

And Mom looked at me sad-like and said, "No, Charlie. More like **fur** in his brain. Maybe the stroke made a wire come loose up there, and now he can't get connected!"

That idea was a little scary to me. "Is that like the wires connecting my eyes, Mom? Do you think I'll have a stroke if one of them comes loose?"

But Mom smiled and said that wasn't the way it worked at all with humans. They weren't wired together like me, just Held Together By The Miracle of God's Grace.

Mom could tell I was disappointed because we had to leave so suddenly. "Sometimes, Charlie, it's better to have a really wonderful time for even a little while, rather than try to force things. I'm hopeful Father will find a lot in common with Stephen. He loved playing with the dogs, and he was drawn to Uncle Ben, so maybe he will open up eventually."

Well, that "open up" stuff didn't sound good to me.

It sounded like something medical. That's something else Mom is really bright about. She's always studying these learned medical books in our room, and she told me one of her ancestors was the first "herb" doctor in the county where we live.

Then, just in case I wasn't confused enough, Mom whispered to me that it wasn't "sheeps" we had just seen; it was "sheep." Mom's not wrong very often, but this time I just knew she was wrong. They were sheeps. After all, I know you say "lamb" if there's only one, and "lambs" if there's more; and "bear" for just me, but "bears" for all my friends in our room. And "human" for one, like Mom, and "humans" when they're more, like Mom and Father.

So how can a whole lot of sheep not be "sheeps?"

Now I **really** had lots of new stuff to think about – Uncle Ben and his magical sounds, baby sheeps that aren't sheeps, and insides of humans with wires connecting their brains. After seeing pictures showing what insides of humans look like, with intestines and stuff like that, I decided to settle for my sawdust-insides.

That's a natural thing, like Big Red's always talking about. Comes from Nature, and the Trees, and the Woods.

18

GETTING HOME FROM SEEING SHEEPS

I know what Mom said about having a really good time, even if it's just for a little bit, but I really didn't want to have to leave Uncle Ben and the sheeps yet, so I tried to move my head so I could see above our car window. That way I could at least watch the little sheeps playing for as long as possible.

Mom took over the driving because it was getting so slick, and because she said she was used to driving on the Big River Hill, but I noticed Father's hands were still holding on so tight to the door they were white, as the car slipped first one way, then another. But it was hard for me to pay any attention to the road, because I kept thinking about all the exciting things that had happened today.

Was I finally going to get my dreamed-of golden furwool suit? But just then I realized something else – here I'd dreamed and dreamed about my golden furwool suit, but now I could hardly think about that, because I kept wondering about Uncle Ben's magical sounds, and how they filled my heart with joy.

But then I thought again about this whole suit situation and this peculiar measurement-stuff going on lately with my body. Suddenly I knew exactly why Mom had such trouble with her measurements of me: they just didn't make any sense! "Arm's-eye to paw;" "naval to crotch;" Barbara'd said. Well, one thing for sure: whoever taught these ladies to sew or knit sure hadn't gone to the same kind of school as my Mom.

And about here I really got discouraged.

I smiled when I looked at Father, still holding on to the door with white knuckles, not saying a word, while the car slid, first one way, then another. Well, Father might not be saying anything right now, but he sure felt something. Tense. I think that's the word.

But, as we crept along, the main thing that kept puzzling me was where I had heard or seen Uncle Ben's magical sounds? And I decided right then that learning about them was something even more important than getting my golden furwool suit I've waited for forever. I truly needed to get to the root of that.

Oh gosh! Here was that word again; has everything got a root? Even me?

I remembered the night when I discovered those awful Scots skirts in one of Mom's books, and Mom tried to reassure me about the outfit she planned for me, saying . . . "we are going to share our roots, Charlie. You're part of my family now, which means we share everything." That sure did sound great, and it made me all warm and happy that Mom trusted and loved me enough to make me part of her family, even if she did think I reminded her of a "stalwart Scots ancestor." I was just one lucky, fifteen inch teddy bear with mesmerizing golden eyes, old red flannel body, no knees and black feet, but I still didn't quite understand what Mom said about our sharing "roots." I wondered if I hadn't used it in the right context?

I guess I had been wool gathering again for awhile, because here we were at home suddenly, and we all got unpacked. "Romantic" candles suddenly appeared on the table for the picnic Mom and Father'd not had time for, and Big Red and I went to our room. And managed somehow to make enough room for ourselves on our chair. It having more or less now been occupied by A. R. – Abandoned Rabbit, Mom named him.

And boy! Is he huge!

About four times bigger than any rightful rabbit ought to be, I guess, me not knowing very many rabbits, or how to measure. But A.R. got outgrown by a granddaughter . . . who was establishing a nest of her own. (Well, why couldn't he live in **HER** nest?) That's what rabbits do, I thought.

But Mom's middle-aged sweet daughter couldn't bear to give him away. So he rode around in her car for a long time, while she tried to give him up. But he had too many sentimental memories attached to him, and so – what else? He ended up at Mom's. On **MY** chair. Where he really is pretty overpowering!

But on nights when Mom opens up our window farther than she should, and tries to save oil by turning down the furnace, he's pretty warm to snuggle up to.

And that's what friends are for, aren't they? Snuggling.

Until I get my furwool suit.

19

GREAT BIG HEAPS

Now that I was beginning to understand just a little about how some words mean the same thing even if they're spelled different, and how some words don't mean what they sound like at all, and some of this more-than-just-plain-peculiar stuff that goes on when you get mixed up with ABC's, just trying to do something Mom calls "broaden your horizons," I thought I was beginning to make some sense out of writing things down so you can teach other people.

I found Mom hadn't learned all this yet.

Just a night or two after we'd been on our trip to The Sheep Farm, and everyone had turned in except Mom, things were quiet and peaceful, Father evidently having been persuaded by the cats that it was time to sleep. I was enjoying listening to his dear little zizzly sounds, when something puzzling about words and spelling fell in on my Mom.

I had been talking with B.R. and my other friends when suddenly a pretty loud statement floated from the living room through the hall. Evidently Mom had reached another talking-to-herself mode.

Lots of paper shuffling, things thumping on the Persian carpet, more papers, more exclamations – then it got totally quiet. I sat there waiting for Mom to come on in, but she didn't for a long time. I was getting really worried when she came in, and finally sat down in an absolute heap on the bed. Much more than the usual **heaps** I'd seen overtake her periodically. A kind of despair heap. Then I saw a few tears come out of her lovely blue eyes, and she turned to me and said, "I tell you, Charlie, that really rocked me back on my heels!"

And I really couldn't understand, because it seemed to me she wasn't on her heels, for Heaven's sake; more like sitting on . . . well, what human-persons sit on, there on the edge of her bed.

Since she still didn't say a word, but kept sort of staring off into space, I thought this was an appropriate time for me to gently remind her that I was her dearest friend, and what were friends for if not to help . . . for that's what she's told me more than once.

Finally, she began to open up. (Mom explained to me recently what "open up" means to humans: it's where the mouth opens, and then all sorts of things begin to spill out, some of them you maybe wish you didn't have to hear.) I wasn't too sure I could cope with whatever this was that had my Mom in such a terrible state.

But when Mom started to tell me, it took me a very long time to put things in their proper perspective, for what she told me didn't seem all that bad.

Mom and Father get huge stacks of mail every day, and she had been too busy to get rid of a lot of junk stuff, so she was trying to catch up, when she suddenly read a pome in one of the magazines, and it got her all upset.

"What did it say?" I asked her.

She told it to me and gosh, it didn't seem that earth-shattering to me, but maybe I wasn't putting it in its proper context. It was just a tiny little pome by a human-person name of Dr. Sooose.

> *...so the writer who breeds*
> *more words than he needs*
> *is making a chore*
> *for the reader who reads.*

I listened real hard, and I could immediately tell that this doctor person was mixed up himself, for he used the word "breeds." Now I know enough to know that "breeds" has something to do with mating for life, like Mom and Father, and kinds of animals like horses, so he needn't have put my dear Mom in such an absolute state of despair!

So I tried to explain this to Mom, even letting out this secret thing I've been able to do lately (like maybe rhyming a thing or two – maybe even sort of a pome). I shared this secret about my words with her, saying

...they just floated away,
like a soft summer's day
© *C. Bear*

Mom got so excited she got a really happy look on her dear face, jumped up, grabbed me from the chair, and said: "Oh, Charlie! I'm so proud of you! That's a **real pome** and I'll write it down for you!"

So I figured this might be the time to mention I'd seen some of her catalogs, and it occurred to me I might be able to really write, not just have to have her help me all the time, because my beautiful golden paws don't have fingers like humans do. "Maybe, Mom," I said, "maybe if I got some rubber stamps with letters on them, and an ink pad, I could really write then."

But she didn't seem to understand what I was trying to say about writing with stamps and pads. Instead, Mom looked at me sort of puzzled funny, and told me she did not know where I got my voice. "I keep listening for some sort of accent, Charlie, but your voice seems to sound just like I sound in my own brain. Does that make sense to you?"

Well, not really, but I certainly didn't want to upset Mom again, since she'd just about gotten over her traumas relative to this Dr.

Sooose person. Once she started explaining, I could see immediately he was talking about something completely different from what Mom and I are writing. His books are for little children, but ours is a real-life adventure story for adults. People just like Mom and Father. And me.

So how much can you condense us without losing our "voice?"

I could see Mom was still pondering this, which seemed impossible to me, so I tried to cheer her up: "Maybe big bear-hug-squeezings from you might condense me?"

Just then – as I was feeling that what I had told Mom was something good and would make her smile again – a strange thing happened and I got a big case of the shivers. Here came some of Uncle Ben's magical sounds, or signs, and they began to float all around us, and Mom looked startled, and I knew she'd been taken aback, and then we both sat down on the bed in a heap. Mom and me, beginning to feel peaceful; enjoying to the uttermost those mystifying, comforting signs. Sometimes they sounded like notes of music, then maybe like something that had never even been written down, just had been there waiting to give us joy. So I told Mom this, and she said something pretty important, but I didn't know then quite what it meant. Like . . . this cord of love which binds us all together, and deep down we know these things, if we are perceptive enough to understand. But life is so hectic, lots of people haven't the time to search for **the true meaning of life**.

Finally she said: "We'll know all these things when we get to Heaven, Charlie, for all things will be made clear then!"

And when she said that, the best smile ever came over my dear Mom's face, and I could see that she was happy. And I hoped we'd **both** be able to find this Heaven, and wouldn't have to condense me.

20

I.N.T.E.R.M.I.N.A.B.L.E.

Every time I thought I was really beginning to understand big human words, Mom would say something and I got lost all over again. Like one of her favorite words – "interminable." Once it got started, Mom said it was an interminable summer! Hadn't seemed that way to me, particularly her having said previously that it was an interminable winter!

And, since one was hot and the other was cold, I couldn't put things in their proper context.

Back in the Winter, Mom had said . . . "we never can GET OUT!" And here Mom and Father were both "out," and it was still **interminable**. "Out" in the gardens seemed way too long to me. For, as I've mentioned, Mom didn't have to try to work up a good sweat. It just seemed to come natural – something about her genes.

I figured Mom had forgotten about "dry cleaning" me after she'd come up with that truly scary-sounding statement Thanksgiving Day. It sure hadn't sounded great, and I couldn't figure out what she meant. One thing for sure, though, if it had anything to do with taking a bath, which seems to be humans' way of getting clean, not swishing and burbling around in some clean mountain stream the way all bears do – then forget it! I'd had something like a bath one time, when cousins came to visit Sally's grandmother, and they went off and left me overnight in the yard, and I fell in a wading pool and thought I'd never get out. But as it turned out, that dry cleaning took care of itself, as Mom explained to a good friend on the phone, in a subdued, stricken, regretful tone of voice the morning after it happened, and said she'd never felt so dumb, and . . . how could she be so forgetful? And a lot of things like that I could have corrected her thinking on if I'd been a vindictive bear, 'cause she doesn't have to try real hard to be forgetful.

It just seems to come natural to her, like sweat.

Anyway, it had been another really hot summer day; a lot of work in this big **enormous** yard we've undertaken to care for when we both know we're too old. Work had pretty well been laid by, showers and naps had gone on for part of the afternoon, supper had come and gone with its rich, yummy smells drifting out from the kitchen onto the back porch. That's where I'd been cooling myself all afternoon on this real comfortable, salvaged wicker rocking chair. (Bought at a real bargain, which is another key word with Mom).

Father is a lot different from Mom on this "bargain stuff." It's real important to him not to cheat the other guy, even if you have to pay him more than something's worth. Mom has told me several times that Father is the most ethical, considerate person she's ever known.

I don't quite understand about this "ethical" stuff, but I understand enough to know it means something like not taking advantage of someone just to have more money for yourself. So that's just one more reason why I really love Father.

Anyway, I sat all evening on this green bargain chair, listening to the chirping crickets. Poor aggravating things! What do they have to be so cheerful about? When winter comes they'll all be frozen stiff. Well, the evening came and went, and I began to hear something rumbling way off in the distance.

Flashes of lightning lit the sky, big enormous breeze coming – and it was **w a y** after midnight. And suddenly I knew!

Charlie got forgotten on the bargain chair.

I couldn't believe it! First the dead of winter, forgotten to die in a cold car; now, forgotten in a bargain chair, and probably to be blown away someplace, and nobody will recognize me, for I don't have a name-tag, and **I can't spell my name or address** to tell them who I am.

And Charlie is never going to find his way home!

Evidently some particularly loud clap of thunder woke Mom. Not Father. He was sleeping peacefully in his beddy-bye, from which the two kitties departed like mad, running pell-mell for the basement as Mom charged through the room, almost tripped over the cats, finally got her act together and was frantically trying to reach the back porch, right through a heavy, locked back door.

To rescue her prized begonias! Not **Charlie**; not the bargain rocker . . . **begonias**!

She didn't even see or recognize me at first I guess, for she was lurching around carrying those pots of begonias, back and forth, putting them under the table. From where, as she straightened up one breathless moment, she coincidentally saw that – **OH**! Here was Charlie still on the chair! Scrunched down as best as Charlie could, under a hand-loomed rug (which normally would have had her quick attention). If it hadn't been for the begonias. She took one startled look. Not apologetic-like. Just startled, as if waking from a dream, which I guess she just had. Grabbed poor Charlie **expediently**, wind blowing the hard rain clear across the porch, which by this time, me being forgotten for so long, had already drowned me!

Ran through the bedroom, in which Father, puzzled-awake, was trying to get his bearings, seeing this **madwoman** tearing through the room – him having turned on the light to see what had become of the kitties after they'd left claw marks on him through the blanket and had now disappeared. He asked in a concerned tone of voice: what was going on?

And Mother answered something to the effect . . . she'd never done such a dumb thing, giving no further clues to Father. Who apparently wasn't too interested anyway, as he lay right back down and turned off his light.

Well, I'm going to do some condensing here, what with the several hours Mom worked really hard trying to dry poor drowned Charlie! Wrapping me in a yummy smelling, big fluffy towel, patting my gorgeous golden head gently, carefully drying my beautiful tender ears, wiping out my mesmerizing golden eyes which, she said, she was afraid might fill with tears and have no place to go! (Oh, **I** had a place to go all right, and it was to **sleep!**)

But that didn't come for awhile, because all of a sudden Mom remembered she used to have a pretty reliable hair dryer; went searching frantically through the linen/sewing closet for it. Left all the lights on in my room, which woke all my friends. But they couldn't say a word for fear Mom would hear, and she would realize they knew what had happened to poor Charlie!

Plugging in that penetrating-sounding, blowing hot-air-thing into an electrical socket while I was still wet! Me reminding her pretty quickly that was **not** a good idea! Mom looking really stricken then, thanking me for reminding her. Me falling asleep finally, wrapped in another clean, dry, yummy smelling, fluffy towel, sleeping on Mom's bed!

Some things are worth all the anxiety they cause, just to get to the end result.

But then there followed the whole second part of this episode the next morning, when I suggested it would be nice to lie out in the lovely warm sun, and maybe that would dry me the rest of the way. If the sun wasn't too hot, and if my old red flannel didn't shrink.

Big stricken look from Mom!

The absolute termination of the episode of the storm got finalized in just a couple more days, when Mom lovingly turned me ever so often on the blanket under the beech tree, where she'd placed me in the filtered sunlight coming through the leaves.

She did mention once during this time absentminded-like, that she thought she had some cornmeal in a big, clean jar, like her Mother used to use on their fur collars – before there were any dry cleaners.

Either she couldn't find it; forgot about it, or decided Charlie was going to dry clean all by himself.

21

SEEDS OR GERMS

Things seem so peaceful now with all the pleasant weather. It's nice just to sit and watch the butterflies, the birds darting around, and lots of things growing. It's true! You can almost see them grow.

We've had lots of things growing this summer in our gardens.

And it seems they come from seeds.

Mom hadn't gone any further with her explanation at the time though and so, being an inquiring bear, trying very hard to add to his knowledge, a bit at a time, I asked her the question about seeds.

"Did I come from a seed too, Mom?" I asked, trying to keep stuff in its proper sequential order. Mom had already told me one time that was where everything came from, including humans.

Well, Mom got sort of a peculiar look, a maybe introspective look? And she said something like . . . "No, Charlie, I guess more like a **germ** of an idea in Mom's fertile brain."

And then she giggled.

Me, not liking the sound of this much, for I know just a little about germs – since I sneaked a peek in some of Mom's big medical tomes – thought I'd like to hear her explanation. And she did try, saying that even the beautiful white dogwood tree, right over our back fence, came from a seed. "But that doesn't mean you can tell anything about how big things are going to turn out, because some of the seeds that grow into the biggest things are very, very tiny!"

Well, since I'm only about fifteen inches tall, but a "**great big bundle of joy,**" to quote Mom, I wondered if the "seed" in her brain had grown into something bigger than she ever expected?

I spent a lot of time thinking about "seeds" and "roots" (another of Mom's expressions). It was really hot, Father and Mom were both pretty weary and beat from the heat and, after a light lunch and their showers, they both stretched out in utter contentment in their big chairs, Mom at one end of her reorganized table (where all my notes and jottings are arranged in neat piles. **By me**.) Then Father moved over to the couch to stretch out in what he calls a supine position, but not before Mom had covered him with a blanket.

Having a pretty active mind – for all bears have to be alert in order to survive – I sort of let my gaze wander first over Mom's Teddy Bear Magazine (and here again, I can tell you, it's really spellbinding!!) And you'd like it too if you're a bear lover, and probably run right out and buy one.

Besides, it has the neatest ads for clothes, and all sorts of appropriate things for bears just like me, who don't have much in the way of a wardrobe. Except the blue and white suit from the Doll Lady that sure looks like jammies to me – and maybe a misguided tar-tan suit hanging in the closet, waiting for an appropriate occasion to wear it. And the promise of a golden furwool suit, which is sure a long time in the making.

Anyway, by this time I had a good deal of confidence in my abilities, and I figured if I had been enterprising enough to talk to this Barbara person and manage to get my message across, maybe it wasn't an utter impossibility to try to order me some more appropriate garments.

Sure, money could be a problem, me not having any. But already understanding all these human-complexities about money, how you don't have to have money, but can call off some felicitous numbers and give the appropriate code – I figured it wasn't any big deal. So **I did it.**

And the order lady on the phone just seemed to know right off what I meant, and when I remembered the numbers Doll Lady and friend Barbara had repeated under their breaths as they categorized me in their little notebooks, I just repeated them with what Mom said later (when she recovered her composure) was surely a great deal of aplomb. I was proud that Mom was so proud of my accomplishments, not even being stumped about ordering overalls for my friend Big Red too.

Although, I have to admit, I **did** have some degree of difficulty with his overall size, until Order Lady said "not to worry. Some bears have longer legs than others." And . . . "I'll just send a size I think is appropriate, then you can hem them up if they're too long." (Which I knew almost indubitably they would be, Big Red having such disproportionate legs. **Stumpy.**)

Then Order Lady said she'd send us a new catalog soon, so that maybe they could help us in the future more expediently.

Oh boy! Wasn't that easy? See what you can do, if you'll just get up off your chair, put one foot in front of the other, and do it?

All this time Father had been making this dear little zizzly-noise he works himself into when he's worn out and falls asleep, and I thought it might be a good idea for **me** to zizzle too before Mom woke up. But of course I couldn't close my mesmerizing eyes, and they were wide open when Mom, with that sixth-sense of hers, suddenly sat straight up, looked all around with this disorganated look she gets sometimes. She asked was I ok, and had I heard the phone ring?

"No," I answered truthfully, having gotten through the very first time on that **eight hundred number**.

Then I wondered what would happen if I dialed those nine hundred numbers I had heard about somewhere. The ones which Mom had told me had **inappropriate** material.

Well, I know about that! There's my tar-tan suit, for instance.

22

GOOSEBUMP WEATHER

One morning, a weather-change seemed to come, with a different-feeling breeze, and Mom said something like, "Oh, Glory! It's almost goosebump weather." And . . . "Just the first morning I've got a spare minute, I'm going to take my T to the back porch, and look all around, and smell the roses. And forget about everything for just a little while!"

And Father made some remark like, "whatever turns you on."

Which seemed incomprehensible to me, but I figured it had something to do with the round thermostat in the hall, which was always being turned on, and turned down, and turned up. And me, not knowing anything about electrical stuff, outside of the fact that you must not plug in or touch the stuff if you're wet like I'd been during that storm (the night when Charlie got drowned).

Anyway, I just stood there real silent-like, having these ponderous thoughts as to how much I was going to reveal in the **next** chapter of my book.

Now, in trying to keep things in **consecutive** order (which is hard if you can't count numbers farther than ten, so it's a pretty big step for me, and I'm really proud of it), some place back, about maybe Fourteen Chapter, Mom says. With us leaving so precipitously from The Sheep Farm, what with the snow, and the lambs coming down, I forgot to mention that Barbara and husband Stephen were going to go on a trip to California. And Barbara was perturbed, she told Mom, because she didn't know what to do about Uncle Ben.

"Here he is, just beginning to put down **roots (??)**, and we'll have to **up-root (??)** him all over again, because we don't know anyone to come in while we're gone," Barbara had said.

And Mom told me she'd been apologetic. Said he was so enchanting that she'd love to have him stay with us, but we just didn't have room. Maybe, Mom said, maybe the nursey home north of here would be nice, and . . . she'd try to keep in touch with him. "Charlie and I can go and visit," she'd said, and lots of comforting things like that.

Well, it turned out that he had gone there, although I didn't know where "there" was, but I could see that it made Father depressed when Mom mentioned that maybe he could go with us? And . . . he might get over his understandable aversion and sadness.

And things like that.

I knew Mom meant well, but here she'd taken on something else. She explained it by saying, "First things have to come first, Charlie."

Even **I** know that, but I wasn't able to put it into the proper context for quite a while.

So maybe we were going to take a trip! But to a **Nursey Home**, which didn't sound too exciting to me. But then Mom tried to help me understand that it wasn't always the exciting things which matter; that Life isn't full of excitement always, but lots of people went around thinking it was and wasting their lives looking for it. Mom said it was important to realize that, when we help our friends, it more than compensates for the lack of excitement. "When you do that, Charlie," Mom said, "it leaves a warm glow that lasts for a **long** time."

And then she picked me up, smiled her sweet, crinkley-cornered, blue-eyed smile, and gave me another of her special hugs.

It was yummy! And it proved once again what I knew the first moment we found each other at the anteek auction: I am one **lucky** bear!

Not only did Mom's comments have a special effect on me, they evidently had the same effect on Father. Later she mentioned that she had hoped maybe he could go with us to lend something she called **moral support,** and that maybe he and Uncle Ben might find something she called a "common cord." Well, Father looked just a little bit interested, and I could see that this maybe touched the cord of compassion Mom had been talking about.

You don't have to go very deep to do that with Father. It seems more a matter of him being too compassionate, and that's the reason things get to him too easily, because he feels sad for people. Too sad, Mom said. And I had trouble putting this in the proper context: Tears-sad? Heart-aching sad? Nostalgic sad? Let's not have depressed-sad!

But I decided I'd do my very best to keep Father from getting that sad, so that evening I told him about the two bears who woke up one morning while they were hibernating.

> *"Is it time to get up?" One of them said to the other.*
> *And the second bear said: "I didn't hear the alarm go off."*
> *Then the other bear said: "What alarm? Did you pack it?"*
> *And the second bear said: "You Dummy! That was your job!*
> *Can't you ever get anything right? Now we'll have to go back to sleep!"*
>
> © *C. Bear*

But I don't know if Father heard me or not. He just sat there with this kind of introspective look in his gentle brown eyes, tilted his head sideways, and looked at me sort of puzzled like.

When I told Mom what had happened with Father, she got excited. Said she was sure he was beginning to hear me. I sure hope so. I'd sure like to learn all about the big important stuff Father knows. Me being a highly intelligent, motivated bear and all.

23

THE NURSEY HOME

"Talk about eye-opening experiences," Father commented when we returned from our first visit to the Nursey Home. "You were right to insist I accompany you." Mom got the most beautiful smile at his enthusiasm for the previously dreaded excursion.

He went on to admit that, while proper care was something he called "essential" for everyone in the home, he thought the most important thing was more a matter of all those folks keeping each other company. Maybe even enjoying exchanging their symptoms, each one being so unique.

Father's enthusiasm made Mom so happy she suggested we should try to set up a regular routine of going there.

Oh oh! That "regular routine" and "organized patterns" of living and stuff like that, always just seem to get away from Mom. It isn't that she doesn't try with all her might, but what with her being so involved in so many things, and somewhat slowing down, organized just seems to be the last thing on her list. But, she's told me, "we can't be all things to all people, Charlie." And she guesses she's too old to change.

But I wouldn't have her any other way, for she's all I've got. And sometimes Father, and sometimes the cats, although the two elderly cats still persist in sneaking into Mom's and my room and sniffing on me when they think no one's looking. They never sniff any of the other bears in our room.

Just Charlie.

I just tell them what they're doing is rude, since I certainly would not think of sniffing them. But I swear they actually smile when I say that, and pretend they don't understand Charlie-talk, which I know **indubitably** they do. But they're old, and they're family too, so I try to overlook this one embarrassing habit they have.

Oh! I just realized I didn't tell you cats plural is now **really** cats plural, for Big Boy, being the lovable, huge creature that he is, has moved in permanently. Although, says Father, we don't know what we're going to do with him when winter begins, because he says we can't bring him in with the other kitties who are so firmly established in their home. Father says maybe he's got such a heavy pelage, or is going to grow one now that winter is coming, that we can make him a nice, warm bed on the back porch. (I asked Mom about the strange-sounding "pelage" word and she explained it means a very thick coat of fur).

Right about here I wondered if **I** could grow some heavy pelage, my forever-awaited golden furwool suit still not having been forthcoming. In fact, just a few days ago, while Mom and Father were working in the garden, and I was resting indoors on the sofa, in strolled Big Boy, realized he and I were all alone in the room, hopped up on the sofa, stretched his **gigantic,** champagne-colored**,** heavy pelaged body on top of my body – and went to sleep!

Actually, he's so huge he didn't just stretch out on my lap, he completely **covered** poor Charlie, who was trying not to suffocate! First Charlie gets left outside to freeze to death, then he almost gets drowned in a storm when Mom forgets him until she remembers her prized begonias – now poor Charlie is about to suffocate because Big Boy, who apparently **loves** Charlie and just wants to be friends, smothers him by lying down on what used to be Charlie's lap – and legs, and chest, and face and . . . .

Fortunately, just as I was getting dizzy from lack of "un-furry air," in comes Father, removes him from what was left of poor smooshed Charlie, and saves the day. But not before Big Boy licks and kisses Charlie on the face, real affectionate-like!

When I regained my composure – and thought about it for awhile – I came to one very important observation. Given a choice between being rudely sniffed by the two elderly cats (who got here first, so I can't complain) and being smooshed and loved to death by Big Boy, I decided I would rather be kissed than sniffed.

I'll bet that's what most humans would choose too, if they had a say in the matter.

―⋘―

Apparently Mom has gotten ahead of herself again, talking about cold weather coming, and goosebumps – because Winter is nowhere near here yet. Here's this gorgeous season they call FALL arriving, and me still with no furwool suit. But even **I** agree things have been hectic, and time has sort of slipped away lately, just like Father and Mom were discussing on the porch today.

Cool Fall breezes greet us when we go outside, and Mom almost has her goosebump weather, and breathes really deeply and happily on the mornings when she is able to get up at a more respectable time. And just about here, Mom suddenly remembers to tell me that friend

Barbara has called and said my **furwool** suit is ready to be tried on! And Mom – although at one time this was the **most important thing** in my life – has forgotten to mention this to me!

But Mom puts me in the car, careful-like, and carefully seatbelts me so I won't be injured, and we make a hurried trip to see friend Barbara, and her sheeps, and my golden furwool suit! When we get there, I slip into the suit, which is not too easy, as it fits me like a glove. But some sort of a catchy-thing called a gripper has zipped me up the back.

Right away Barbara and Mom agree there are some problems to be taken care of so Charlie's new furwool suit will be just perfect: my golden furwool suit seems to be too low down, and it puckers a little, and needs to be un-done and adjusted.

Barbara scratches her head and says "I don't know how I could have miscalculated that length!" Well, even though I still have trouble with wunz and truze, I am proud to say I can now carefully count to ten. I know what the problem is: she didn't get the right numbers.

So Mom, being the comforting, reassuring soul she is, says something like "I know it has been an imposition on you, and Charlie has his overalls now, and they're more appropriate for our gardens . . ." and some more stuff along that line, which evidently lets Barbara be something Mom calls "off the hook," and after a short visit and more fun watching lots of sheeps, we go back home.

Still no suit for Charlie. Just friendly reassurances. But at least Mom didn't blab about how we got my overalls, although it seemed to me there was some mention about things getting out of hand again. And, of course, while we'd been gone, Mom had gotten behind on something else, and practically ran out the door to do that, while I was trying to remind her about the catalog which the order-lady had kept her promise on and sent with our overall order.

So it seemed to me this might be a more expeditious way to arrive at my wardrobe. I got really excited when I thought I'd even seen little pairs of boots, and I sort of shuddered if Mom ever got the idea she could whip those up on her new sewing machine she's so proud of (but has yet to use to make clothes for Father or Charlie)! So, while I longed to get this whole project finished, I decided I'd better just let things go along as they were, for **I n d u b i t a b l y** Mom thought she was following the write root!

Finally here came this gorgeous Fall weather that Mom loves so much. The leaves turned brilliant colors, lots of friends and relatives descended to enjoy them. And lots more food, and more reorganizing our time, and stretching things to the limit. And here came Mom's birthday, with her trying her best to ignore it. But both her daughters and granddaughter brought presents and made a big cake with her favorite icing and some homemade ice cream. And then Father gave Mom this gorgeous red, sparkley thing on a chain to hang around her neck, and Mom got all warm and glowey like the leaves, telling him he shouldn't have spent so much. But Father just smiled, happy-like.

But all this made me sad, because I didn't have anything for Mom. Again. (I hadn't known you were supposed to do that, me never having had a birthday of my own.) So Charlie felt inadequate. And sad. Not depressed-sad, just realistically-sad, particularly because Mom seemed to think if she'd ignore her birthdays from now on, she wouldn't get any older. Well, I know you can try as hard as everything to ignore things, but some things are just **inevitable**.

Just about then Mom realized that I was sad because I didn't have any present for her. "Oh, Charlie," Mom said later when we were getting ready to go to sleep, "there are many kinds of gifts people

— and very special bears like you, Charlie — give each other. You've already given me the best birthday gift I could ever ask for."

"What, Mom?" I asked, confused about what she was trying to say.

"You've helped me see the world with entirely new eyes!" She said, picking me up and giving me several of her most yummy hugs. Fortunately, Big Red was in the other room, Mom having brought him there to watch another basketball game with Father that evening; otherwise, he might be jealous of all the hugs Mom gave me, and I didn't want that.

Then one morning, shortly after her big, momentous birthday, Mom said she could just lie down under our old, gnarled Beech tree because it was such a gorgeous, glowey morning. And Father surprised me — and Mom too I think — by saying why didn't she? And she said she believed she would, but didn't stay there very long before she said something about getting a painting started before the leaves were all gone. And I know she didn't have time to paint another picture, and I think Father knew that too. But she's been working so hard all summer, and getting so hot, and sort of depressed at how little she thinks she's been accomplishing, so we didn't say anything to her. Just let her begin squeezing out some of those colors Mom calls "glorious" from their tubes.

But that wasn't all: Mom decided that, maybe to justify some of the anxiety "I've put Barbara through . . . making that suit for Charlie . . ." (?? What suit??) . . . "I believe I'll finish that sketch I started of the meadow and the sheeps under the tree."

And darned if she didn't finish it, and it was great! Even Father gave Mom lots of compliments. And it seemed then like some great big weight of a thing had been lifted from her shoulders because she'd accomplished something! And Father and I both got several hugs, and that was really great. But there wasn't any mention about my book, and I couldn't figure out how I was ever going to finish it unless Mom helped me, since I can't type, and I still haven't figured out how to use that tape-thing Mom's never been able to master herself.

But then I thought: machines aren't that big a deal. After all, I had managed to use the phone to order overalls for me and Big Red, and to call friend Barbara. So, that morning when Mom was busy making piccalilli from all the leftovers in the garden – green tomatoes, and peppers and onions and spices – and while a lot of good yummy smells were coming from the kitchen, I decided I'd try to use some of the blank tapes Mom had left lying there, all neat in a little box.

I tried one out on the radio-recorder-alarmed-clock thing sitting on her work-table by the bed. But it seemed there was already a symphony or something like music on it, and I'd not known that, and among all the notes from some ethereal instruments played by unseen persons with a lot of expertise, here came Charlie's voice, sort of. And maybe some of Uncle Ben's beautiful sounds?

And me, not knowing anything at all about volume, and the proper button to control it, here came Mom, thinking she'd finally figured out how to set the alarmed clock thing on the radio to turn on music, and saying . . . "Well, I guess I got that licked!"

Stopping short when she reached the room and saw the alarmed clock wasn't playing music after all, because the radio part wasn't on! Not being able to figure this out; just erasing the event from her mind as another mysterious thing, and going back to the piccalilli making.

But as I sat and thought about it, and tried to figure out in my mind just what all the buttons, and numbers and code-things were on that thing, I decided I hadn't completely failed. At least I'd got up from my chair, put one foot in front of the other, and **tried**!

And that's about all you can expect from a highly motivated, middle-aged bear who's only learned to count to elevenses!

24

SOOOSA MARCHES

Things didn't change too much for the better around home in the coming days – not organized better – anyway. But happy – better seemed to be all around us, for evidently Mom felt Father had accomplished an awful lot this summer.

And she told him this frequently, particularly if she thought he was about to get depressed again. I know I've already shared with you what a beautiful, almost glowey smile my Mom gets when she is happy, but have I told you about Father? When he smiles, it's like a lightbulb comes on, sending beams of happiness all around the room. We've had a lot of those beams recently, even when we go to the Nursey Home, which Mom thought might depress him.

According to Father, he's conquered his aversion to going where Uncle Ben is living. And basically Father, being such an intelligent, caring human being, enjoys sitting quiet-like and talking to some people up there who don't have anybody at all left in their families. Mom says it's helped him "find his voice" at last (although I never found out where it had been lost). Anyway, all in all, it seems Father has made a big hit! And, I guess, so have I!

Although, maybe I shouldn't mention it; but it's not bragging, is it, to state that I made an awful lot of friends that summer? I could hardly believe how tickled they were to see me, most of them having moved to the Nursey Home in such a hurry. Over and over they'd tell Father and Mom and me their kids had taken over their house, and got rid of all their bears and favorite possessions, and heartbreaking things like that which led, I guess, to these folks being more than usually appreciative of this warm, loving Charlie.

Who was still traveling to the Nursey Home in what sure seemed to me to be a jammy outfit for a doll! Suit of gold not having yet been forthcoming. But when I asked Mom about "forth-coming" and if it came after wunz and truze, she said we'd left out **threez**. And a bunch more stuff explaining that **forthcoming** word. That I didn't get, not having been taught to count yet. (Maybe **that's** forth-coming?)

My overalls were so dirty Mom said she couldn't believe it! So she helped me remove them and placed them with the other dark things to wash separately, so they wouldn't fade.

No panic here though, on Mom's part. But panic from me: no; more like **despair**, with me just longing and longing all this time for my golden furwool suit so I could be appropriate, not still going visiting to the Nursey Home in my jammies, for gosh sakes.

But Mom said they were appropriate, since many of the nursey people had on robes and jammies, and that gave her another idea: to create something she called a "debonair look" for me. Like Clark Gable had, she said, him lounging around in his silk pjs in the movies. So she got one of "Dad's least favorite ties," cut off the end, folded it around my neck, and tucked the ends under my jammy-jacket. When I looked in the mirror I was pretty surprised, for it finally covered the gap between my red-flannel chest and where the jammy-jacket didn't meet.

However. It seemed that this "least favorite tie" of Father's hadn't been categorized properly, it having cost an "arm and a leg," being pure silk. But patient, forgiving Father evidently accepted the inevitable, and I suppose realized that Mom would **never** be able to sew the tie back together on her new, "really bargain" sewing machine.

Father, with that sweet look he gets sometimes in those brown eyes, went on to other matters. But not before saying something pretty forcefully about Mom **not** touching those authentic tar-tan shorts she got for him years ago. And Mom, suddenly looking worried, went quietly to her dusting-cloth bag, rummaged around in there, and triumphantly placed those shorts in the washing-hamper, where she told me she'd have to wash them soon before he missed them.

Despite the fact lots of things hadn't gotten done yet, Mom had managed to fill our freezer, what with Father having reaped such a magnificent harvest . . . "this very first summer you tried!" And then a big hug would come along when she'd say that, and I really liked to watch those!

There were several evenings now, what with the cool breezes blowing across our back porch, when Mom would go out sometimes, I guess looking for that goosebump weather, and sit drinking her T with such a happy look as she talked to Father – and sometimes to a neighbor who'd call across our fence – that I figured goosebump weather must be a very splendid, happifying thing.

And then **I** got **goosebumps**! And knew immediately what Mom had been talking about. (Although she had explained to me previously, it had nothing to do with geese, but came sometimes from sudden drops in the temperature, or what she called "a great big thrill," reminding you of something deep down.)

For all of a sudden that evening, from way off somewhere, I heard drums and horns, and my **Sooosa** March! And here came goosebumps for **me**! For I thought maybe my Sally was there just waiting for me, wherever that music was. And although I knew it had been a long, long time, I knew I'd know her sweet little face anywhere!

Up until then Big Red, and Father and Mom and I had been sitting on the back porch, until Mom had said dinner was almost ready, "but I sure hate to go in." But they had worked all day grinding special meat and making some kind of little noodle packages for the meat and spices to make something called "kreplac," which was one of Father's very favorite dishes. So they went inside to partake while Big Red and I stayed outside on our chairs.

Marvelously coincidentally about this time, our young neighbor Kevin and his Patches-cat came along through our back yard, Kevin wheeling his shiny bike, Patches riding in the basket on the back. Patches looked pretty aggravated when she saw Big Boy, still occupying **HER** porch. But without Father there to invite her inside, she scrunched back down in the basket, resigned to a ride with Kevin.

It was then I saw there was room for me in the basket. And maybe they were going wherever that goosebump music was coming from, and maybe I'd just hitch a ride. And Patches said "o.k."

And Kevin didn't realize I was going, let alone that I wasn't supposed to leave home without telling Mom where I was going. So he didn't notice when I just gave a roll, tumbled into the basket with Patches, and away we went. On the trail of that music!

And maybe, my Sally!

25

BAD THINGS CAN HAPPEN TO GOOD PEOPLE – AND TEDDY BEARS

This "Band Concert" thing evidently wasn't far away, for the music quickly got louder and louder. And more goosebumps popped out, and I thought maybe at last I was going to have tears roll down my cheeks, for such a longing filled my heart I thought I'd weep!

But they didn't; that much hadn't changed about me. Then the lights got brighter. Not just the street lights hanging, swaying in the soft, late-summer breeze, but big, enormous lights on tall poles appeared, and lots of cars were there, and loud, shouting people. And kids marching around in long, wavy lines on a big field, while a man with a big horn yelled at them in frantic, unintelligible words.

A lot of interested human-persons were sitting around, some of them in cars, some of them on the ground on blankets. And dogs were running around barking, unattended. And the kids' thermometers apparently were stuck like Mom's, for the sweat was really pouring off them as they banged on those great big drums and blew those goosebumpy-notes out of big gold horns!

All of a sudden Kevin stopped, tipped the bicycle on its side, and took off to visit with the other interested spectators. So Patches and I, summarily having no place to go, went down onto the ground! All in a heap!

But Patches-cat, having had years of experience climbing trees (probably to escape unfriendly big dogs), took off for the nearest tree, and that left poor Charlie with no transportation, and no place I could see that was safe. Then I heard this terrible growling noise, and the next thing I knew, I was flying through the air several times, being dropped, grabbed by my little tender ears, then flying again! And some expletive idiot-human was laughing about the big dog playing with a bone! (And that was **ME!**)

And I thought maybe, if I was lucky, I might land on top of one of the cars, or up in a tree with Patches as I sailed again.

But suddenly, as I fell down again through the air, I found myself landing on something soft and warm, and a funny little spoosh-sound came out of this thing.

And I looked into the tear-filled eyes of a tiny little baby-person! Much smaller than any of the other little persons I'd ever met before.

Dirty little cheeks, yellow curls all wet with sweat, and I guess tears. And its little hands were waving around frantic-like. And as I looked right into its little blue eyes, I remembered that fear-dream I'd had years before when I'd seen this big Bear and had no one to protect me. So I looked right back with my steadfast gold eyes – into baby's eyes – and I didn't know what on earth to do!

And then something Mom called a **providential thought** came to me, and as the great big dog made another dash at us, I gathered up my courage, and made the biggest, frowniest, scowliest look I could manage – like a big, mean real bear! And I looked right into the big dog's teeth!

Evidently this was so unexpected, that he stopped in his tracks, cocked his head to one side, then sort of tucked his plumey tail between his back legs – and trotted off!

So, here we lay. All in a roll on the ground, me on top. This smelly, wet, miserable little baby-thing, and one extremely consternated, exhausted, frightened teddy bear with one very tender ear!

Then a shadow came between me and the lights, and I heard this familiar voice: my Mom! But most of the words weren't familiar coming from my Mom's very **stern** looking mouth (which almost all the time I've gotten used to seeing all smiley and loving.) Mom leaned down and started to pick me up, and then the strangest look came over her face, and her mouth opened, but no sounds came out. And she sat down on the ground all in a heap, right beside this little thing and me.

Suddenly I heard sirens, and lots of other scary sounds, and people began to run around, and some of them circled all around us. Then somebody let out a yell. Then another Mom-person sat down right beside us and began to cry. And gathered up the little baby-thing in her arms. And began to rock back and forth, and smooth down its hair, and kiss its little dirty pink cheeks.

Just about then my Mom put her arms around both of them, and I about got squeezed to pieces in between all these excited, happy persons. Well, I guess they were happy, but it was hard to tell, because they were crying too.

That's when Mom told me "baby Jeremy" had toddled off all by himself, right across this dangerous street, trying to find the music. Just like me! And nobody knew where he was, which didn't surprise me because I hadn't heard many intelligible sounds coming from that little quivery mouth – just "Waaaaha." So I thought it was probably beyond his capabilities.

But Mom explained lots of things to me after we got home, while she was cleaning me up and gently rubbing my one very tender ear.

According to Mom this little baby-thing and its Mommy were just moving into our neighborhood, so she left him in his playpen while she was busily unpacking things. And he turned out to be a lot smarter than she thought, because he managed with his little determined hand to undo the safety hook on the pen – and away he toddled – right across the dangerous street. Looking for that music!

So, as I sat there safe and warm and loved in Mom's arms at the end of that scary evening, I decided one thing: that in spite of the awesome schedule God is burdened with, trying to keep humans on the right track, evidently He had time this night to shelter a lost baby and one **very** grateful teddy bear.

Later Mom said she'd scolded me so because she loved me so much. "I was so concerned, Charlie! I didn't know where on earth you'd gone to. I even thought maybe somebody had kidnapped you because you're so unique."

Mom continued to try to explain better to me just what was wrong with my going off without telling anybody where I was going. "There are so many terrible things that can happen, Charlie, because there are so many" . . . expletive-sounding word – surely not said by my Mom – "**ignorant** fools, just waiting for an opportunity to do bad things!"

By the time we arrived home we were pretty breathless. Me from trying to absorb all this bad stuff, and Mom, breathless from hurrying, trying to find me, now all glowey and happy because of baby Jeremy's rescue.

Surprisingly, Mom was not upset too much about my jammy suit, which was torn from the dog's teeth. She hugged me again, saying "I can fix that tear easier than the tears in my heart when I think what could have happened to you, Charlie!"

But the biggest surprise of all was Big Red, sitting on our chair, expectantly waiting for us. He looked smug, which surprised me, because I thought he was my good friend and would be glad I'd been rescued! And I wondered what jealousy was, and wondered if this is what made him look that way?

Then I wondered if it was because of something Father had said when he called me a "hero?"

26

SALLY IS A SEMI-ANTEEK TOO

"Charlie," Mom said the next afternoon, after she had removed my jammy suit so she could repair the little tears. She had wrapped me in my piece of genuine Scots wool and fastened it with her special anteek thistle pin, so I guess she thought I wouldn't feel suddenly naked.

Always thoughtful. That's my Mom. Although most bears, being that they are bears, don't wear any clothes. But I had gotten used to wearing clothes by now, even if I still didn't have my forever-awaited-made-special-for-Charlie golden furwool suit.

I was just about drifted back into sleep when Mom said my name, because she was massaging my ear again, which was still very tender from all the traumas of the evening before. And because Charlie, being a semi-anteek bear, and not a young bear like he used to be, was pretty exhausted from all the excitement.

"Are you happy living here with Father and me?" Mom asked me suddenly. I had never seen Mom look so sad.

"Of course," I replied, surprised my Mom would ask such a question. "I bet I'm the luckiest bear in the whole world to have you for my Mom. And Father too, even though I hope it won't be much longer before he and I can really begin to communicate about big important stuff lots better, me being an intelligent, highly motivated bear and all."

"I even love our cats, although I still think they're awfully old not to know better than to sneak in our bedroom when you're not looking, and sniff me. That's why Big Boy and I get along so much. He just kisses me and smooshes me with his big, **he-mongous** body. But he never sniffs Charlie rudely."

Mom smiled real big when I said that, and I felt better. I sure didn't want my Mom upset with Charlie. Ever.

"If you hadn't rescued me at that anteek sale, I would probably still be stuck in that old cardboard box, or thrown in the trash!"

Mom sat there real quiet-like for such a long time I began to get worried. Something was wrong with my Mom, and it was all Charlie's fault.

"Father and I puzzled and puzzled about how you got off the chair on our porch into that bicycle basket with Patches, Charlie. Did Kevin pick you up and put you there?"

"Oh no, Mom!" I said, not understanding how my getting into the basket was any big deal. "I asked Patches if I could go with him to the Sooosa Music and he told me it was okay, and Kevin had laid his bicycle down on its side against the porch, so I just did exactly what you've told me to do in order to accomplish anything in this life. I just got up off my chair, put one foot in front of the other, and **DID IT!**"

Astonished look from Mom. More silence like her mental gears were working real hard to process everything I was trying to explain to her.

"You've gone with me to some band concerts before," Mom said finally, "so I don't understand why it was so important for you to go all by yourself last evening. It was such a dangerous thing to do, Charlie. I was worried sick, even though it turned out you were truly a hero to scare away the big dogs and save baby Jeremy."

"I got the goosebumps like you talk about, when I heard that Sooosa music playing. I thought maybe my Sally was there, and I just **had** to see her little face again. It's been a long, long time since we were together, but I'd know her sweet smile anywhere."

"If you had found your Sally, Charlie, would you have wanted to leave Father and me and all your friends here, and go live with her?"

Mom was asking me really tough questions and I wanted to give her the <u>right</u> answers. Sally was my first Mom, but she was a little girl, and I hadn't seen her since shortly after that manufacturing-cheepie borned me. I was living with my **REAL AND FOREVER MOM** right now. She had rescued me from that awful cardboard box. She loved me. She was my dearest friend and was teaching me all kinds of really interesting stuff, me being highly motivated to learn all about big, important matters so I can be erudite too.

While I was trying my utmost to answer her in a proper context, Mom asked me another question which really rocked me back on my heels. "Charlie," she asked, with a really strange look on her face. "I know numbers and counting are still a problem for you, but can you tell me how many years old you think Sally is today?"

Well, I tell you, that was a really important question, so I thought and thought, 'cause I didn't want to say anything to make my Mom think I was stupid or anything, me still having difficulties with numbers and all that. And I was worried Mom would be disappointed in Charlie if I could not answer her correctly.

Finally, Mom went to our closet, reached high up for a book with lots of pictures and old pieces of paper which had yellowed. She brought it back to the couch and wanted me to look at it with her. There were lots of pictures of a cute little baby, and some more of a little girl with curly blonde hair – maybe even about my Sally's age.

And lots of pictures of a pretty dark-haired woman and a handsome man smiling, holding the little girl or playing with her in the yard or on some swings.

The little girl was my Sally's age.

The pretty couple was just about the same age as Sally's parents were. I'll tell you, I was truly mesmerized by the photos Mom was sharing with me. I could tell it was really big important stuff and I wanted to know all about it.

Just then Mom turned to another page, and I got the goosebumps all over again. There was the little girl with an old woman, just like Sally's grandmother was. And they were sitting at a little table with some dolls on a porch, having a T party. And then Mom showed me one more page and suddenly I didn't just have goosebumps, I got the **shivers.** Here was a handsome young soldier person holding the little blond-headed girl. He was laughing and pointing at the camera. He looked just like my Sally's father did, when he left for the WAR EFFORT.

Mom closed the book for a minute and put it down on the couch. Then she picked me up and gave me one of her most beautiful, most special hugs yet, so I knew Charlie had not disgraced himself by looking for his Sally last night.

"Charlie," Mom finally said, smiling, "the little girl in all those photos is Peggy, our oldest daughter, when she was a little girl."

"And the young man and woman holding her and playing with her, Charlie, is Father and me."

Well, I'll tell you, I was speechless at this big, important information my Mom had shared about my family with me. I couldn't stop thinking about the pictures. But Mom was still talking, so I needed to listen real careful-like to be sure I put everything I was learning in its proper context.

She opened her special photo book again. She pointed to the little girl with the old woman. Mom's eyes were suddenly wet with tears. "That was my mother, Charlie, with our daughter when she was a little girl. And this," she said, pointing to the handsome young soldier man, "was my brother-in-law, her uncle. They were very close."

"How come I haven't met him before, Mom" I asked, trying to grasp all this big, momentous news Mom was sharing with me. "Does he live a long ways from here?"

Just then Mom's eyes got a sad, far away look. "He lives in Heaven now, Charlie. He died a few years ago." She pulled a photograph from an envelope in the back of the book. It was a picture of a smiling older man. "This picture of him was taken shortly before he died."

I stared at the photograph. He didn't look anything like the first photo of him.

I couldn't help myself. My lip quivered. "Does this mean my Sally is old now too, Mom?"

Mom just nodded.

I suddenly understood what Mom was trying to tell me. All the time I was stuck in that cardboard box in Sally's grandmother's dark attic, becoming a semi-anteek in the process, my Sally was getting older, becoming a semi-anteek as well, maybe even marrying and having children of her own. Maybe even **grandchildren**, like Mom and Father's younger daughter has.

My Sally might even be in Heaven now. Big tears ran down to my insides and I held my Mom real close.

I was one lucky teddy bear to have been rescued providentially by my wonderful Mom who loved Charlie and only wanted him to be happy – and safe.

I finally grasped everything Mom was trying to explain to me and was able to put it in its proper context. Even though Sally was my first owner, that was a long time ago, when she was a little girl. Just like Charlie, she was a semi-anteek now, as old as one of Mom and Father's two daughters.

My Sally knew Charlie got left in a cardboard box with poor Squirrely and melted candles and an old egg beater upstairs in her grandmother's attic. She knew where Charlie was but never came to get him and take him home again with her.

"I love you Mom," I finally said, my lip quivering, as Mom hugged me all tight and comforting.

"I love you too, Charlie."

"You're my 'now and forever Mom,'" I said. And we just sat there all warm and loved and happy.

27

MOM'S PERFECT GOLDEN BEAR

Finally, Mom got herself up that big, **momentous** morning when we were actually going out to friend Barbara's Sheep Farm to get my forever-awaited golden suit! And I couldn't understand – although I should have by now – why Mom wasn't full of enthusiasm. But she hugged me and reminded me again that, unlike Father, she just wasn't a morning person, and she couldn't "get going" until she had her two mugs of T.

Well, **I** sure was "going," all packed and ready, and wearing my cape over my striped jammies, determined to look stalwart, with my debonair tie-thing around my neck. Trying particularly hard to look **appropriate**, while having serious doubts we were ever going to leave. I guess I was just doing something Father calls "borrowing trouble," because first I thought maybe the car wouldn't start, or Mom wouldn't start, or maybe even something I'd heard about called moths might have eaten my golden suit in the interim, it having been in the process so long.

Finally, we were on our way, Father having transported a roll of Mother's beautiful hand-loomed rugs to the car, since she was planning to sell them to an anteek dealer friend after we got my golden suit and visited the sheeps again.

As I looked back at Father, he had picked up Big Boy on the porch, and was helping him pretend to wave with his giant paw!

Mom just smiled when I told her what Father was doing, then proceeded to take off at what seemed to be an excessive rate of speed, evidently having forgotten all about those dangerous galoops she'd warned me about, who drive too fast on our beautiful, windy roads and can cause bad accidents.

Things were peaceful and nice at the Sheep Farm, and there was this extremely loving exchange of hugs and expressions of affection – and Barbara expressing her gratitude for Mom and Father and me visiting Uncle Ben at the Nursey Home while they were gone.

"I understand you, young man, have become quite a hit with many of the residents there," Barbara said, picking me up and giving me a squeeze of affection.

I don't know if teddy bears can blush or not, but my face felt real hot from all the praise and signs of affection friend Barbara was giving me.

While Barbara was hugging me, Mom told her she needed to go back to the car to get a little something for Barbara. And her going back to the car went smoothly, having expeditiously packed this "something" the night before so she wouldn't forget it.

The minute Mom went out the door, this dear Barbara looked in my eyes and said something like: "I'll bet I know someone who's just **dying** to try on his suit!"

Well, not that extreme terminology, I wouldn't think. More like frustrated. Disbelieving that it's finally finished. More like that on Charlie's part. And here she came from the other room, golden furwool suit in hand – and away I slid down into that suit.

My forever awaited, beautiful, golden furwool suit! Made special just for Charlie. All matchey-all-over I was, from my gorgeous golden head, clear down to my old black feet!

If I could, I would have clapped my hands in joy, for I could tell I was finally handsome, just like I wanted to be for Mom and Father. No more old red flannel to apologize for. No more Charlie trying to project a stalwart, **determined** image while wearing doll jammies in public. I looked at myself in the mirror.

Mom's perfect golden bear!

Finally! My suit fit to a T, snug as a bug in a rug (an expression I still don't quite understand but which Mom uses a lot), warm and glowing all the way from my heart, clear through my being, I glowed. I'd have purred if I'd been a cat, and I could hardly wait for Mom to see this finally accomplished project.

No sooner had I thought that than Mom came in, took one look at me, and the warmest, most wonderful smile came over her dear face. She looked at Barbara, and then at me again, and said: "You've just worked a miracle, my friend! I didn't think we could do it!"

Then some consultation went on about a few "minor things." Like . . . maybe Mom had better see about my feet after we got home. Barbara said something very confusing to me that if she'd knitted the feets too, it might have looked like "Dr. Denton sleepers!" And with that they both went into something Mom later told me was the "girlish giggles," which concerned me a bit because I thought Dr. Denton might be a cohort of Dr. Sooose! And I surely didn't want Mom having traumas and depressions because of that silly Sooose pome again.

Then, while I was continuing to admire myself, Barbara said something about wanting to help Charlie maintain his unique, mature individuality. "We don't want any ridicule of his wonderful personage!" And a couple more remarks like that which I pondered on for a good while.

Quite suddenly, with a startled look on her face, Mom exclaimed something about how time flies, then tore the wrapping off this painting she'd created for Barbara and Stephen, sort of tentatively held it out. Well, Barbara smiled about as big as I'd ever seen her, looking at the painting. And immediately took off for the other room! Which seemed odd to me, so I wondered if she was just trying to be polite and wasn't really all that thrilled. That made me feel really bad for Mom, for I knew how many hours of love had gone into it.

But I was wrong to be worried. Talking all the way, and smiling all over, here came Barbara back from the other room with a hammer in one hand, and a couple of nails.

And I was frightened to see her talking around the nails which she'd stuck in the corner of her mouth, since both her hands were full, what with the painting and the hammer. I most emphatically did not think those nails were in a very safe place, and I wanted to mention this to her in no uncertain terms, but as my Mom says, sometimes it's better to keep your mouth shut when you don't know how what you say will be received.

Nails in her mouth and all, Barbara immediately made for a certain spot "where I'm going to hang it, so I can look at it from my favorite chair all the time."

I was so happy Barbara was happy, 'cause I knew how much it pleased my Mom.

So Charlie, who was only trying to be considerate for the safety of friend Barbara – with dangerous nails in her mouth – didn't say a word. Or remind Mom right then that probably my feets could be covered appropriately with those black boots I'd seen in the Bear-Supply-Company-Catalog. That way we wouldn't have to get tangled up with this Dr. Denton person.

Mom's painting went on the nail perfectly, right where Barbara'd meant to put it, and they didn't say anything more about my suit, or me, for Mom remarked suddenly that we had to get going, because "the weather doesn't look too promising!"

And so we did. Leave, that is. Me again enjoying looking at all the sheeps everywhere. Most of all, me thinking happily as I sat there gold all over, perfectly matching my mesmerizing gold eyes, that all those long months of promising about my suit, had finally come to an **interminable fruition**!

28

ONE ALONE TO CALL MY OWN

Mom's always talking about "not getting ahead of yourself." Although I still don't quite understand the rightful meaning of that expression, I understand enough to know I don't want to do that, excited as I am to share some more big momentous moments in Mom's and my life.

But I do want to tell you that, pretty soon after we left The Sheep Farm, me in my terrific fur-all-over suit, Mom intent on getting to this shopping place so she could also become outfitted in some more appropriate clothes – this wonderful thing happened!

We barreled along on the cut-through road Mom knows about, at what I felt might be an excessive rate of speed, but then I might be wrong again, me still not having ridden too much in cars. Except with Mom and Father. And most of the time they drive real careful-like, so as not to be run over by the galoops (which apparently exist on almost every road).

Almost immediately we did arrive at Mom's clothes destination. She locked me in the car, "so no one will steal you, Charlie," and then she took off at what was an excessive rate of walking for Mom, heading for this Mall thing.

I'll confess I was pretty pleased with everything that had happened already this day, my suit having turned out so magnificently, and fitting me like a glove, so I just sort of sat there, smiling all over, knowing soon I would even have those neat-looking black boots from the catalog to complete "my perfect look." Plus, I was looking at all the people who were hurrying, apparently to buy things because it was almost time for another Holiday. And that made Charlie smile some more, because this Christmas I already had a **big**, **momentous** surprise present for Mom, and I knew it would make her so happy I just smiled all over thinking about it. And how hard Charlie had worked to make this wonderful present for his Mom.

Well, this time Mom wasn't gone very long before she came hurrying out with a few packages and tossed them in the back seat. Where the roll of rugs was. Which she stated had to be taken to the Anteek Mall, and disposed of before she changed her mind and gave them to "her girls" and friends for Christmas.

Then she said (and I could hardly believe it) she was getting apprehensive about the weather, because it looked like it was going to snow! And just about the time those apprehensive-words came out of her worried mouth, it did begin.

Just little, pretty flakes, though, and I mentioned to her that it was, I thought, a long way off from those roads becoming **impassable.** (Which seems to be a completely different word from **impossible.** Although as near as I can tell they only have slightly different spellings. Oops! I almost gave away one of my secret presents for Mom.)

We hurried across town, cold wind blowing, skies beginning to darken, Mom worrying some more about getting home, me trying to reassure her that surely it wouldn't get that bad, that fast. Hurried. Hurried. Arrived "there."

I saw this huge, red brick building, where Mom had a really difficult time parking close-by. She quickly got the roll of rugs, mentioned something vague to me about "... only take a minute, Charlie, so ... I think I'll leave the car ..." something she called "running." And I hoped it wouldn't run **too** fast, because Mom can't, and I had visions of her running on her bad feet ... trying to catch the car. Which I didn't quite understand, and it's a good thing I didn't. For what transpired in just a few minutes, while I sat there in a golden glow, nice and warm in my wonderfully splendid furwool suit, led me to believe that I had completely the wrong context of the "car-running" bit!

All of a sudden I could see that Mom's worst apprehension had begun to come true. While she'd been in that big building, the snow descended! From the skies, all over everything, in an out-of-season deluge. It fell down. All at once. And the skies, now having nothing white up in them anymore, got very dark. And the wind blew, and then suddenly, in trying to see out my window, I guess I leaned on something that made the car run, for my window suddenly ran – clear down – and I could see out **too well**!

And the snow began to blow into the car, and suddenly I got just a glimpse of something truly heart stopping – in the big window straight ahead of me in the big shop! But my vision was almost instantly blocked, for in leaning out the window, **I fell out**! Face down, into the white snow. "**Now** you've done it, Charlie Bear," I thought! And ... "I guess I'll lie here and freeze. Although, maybe, my beautiful, made -special for Charlie, furry-suit will protect me adequately until my Mom comes back out and rescues me."

But she didn't.

And Charlie felt truly humiliated lying face down on the snowy sidewalk, unable to get back up.

Suddenly, this kindly-looking man came out of the shops going to his car, and saw me lying there. Not knowing where I'd come from, he must have decided I was an anteek too, so he carried me up the steps, and put me on a long anteek bench, which was providentially placed under the big, frosted, display-window of the Anteek Mall.

And then – I could see! For as I leaned against that frosted glass, and pressed my face (well, mainly my heart-shaped nose, it sticking out ahead of my eyes and mouth . . . which is normal even for bears, not only humans). And I expect that sentence is irrationally arranged, for by this time I saw what I thought I'd seen – from the car!

There in a baby buggy, looking at **me**, was this dear little **girl-bear**! And I knew she was a girl, for she had on a frilly lace hat. And nothing else. Except her beautiful, golden, longer-hair-than-mine body.

And I just stood there, my heart-shaped nose against the glass. All warm with **love**!

And I knew suddenly why I'd been lonely months ago that day at the shop, when Mom had left me in the car, and I'd had my first glimpse of the other little girl-bear in small, squeaky-voiced-person's arms.

I'd been waiting for love!

Not the kind of love which Mom (and maybe Father sometimes) gives me, relentlessly and comfortingly, every day. A different kind of love: a lonely dispelling, searching-for-mate kind of love!

And I thought my heart would burst!

Then suddenly the big front door to the anteek shop opened, Mom came barreling down the steps, not seeing me, heading for our car, opened its door, and looked completely taken aback! Threw some stuff in the car, began to talk to herself (which I could tell, because her mouth was moving). But I could hear no sounds coming out, the wind making so much noise, and blowing big swirls of snow all around.

Then, after considerable frantic looking, Mom found me. She grabbed me, over my most violent protestations, because I'd tried to point out to her why I did **not** want to leave that bench. But I guess she still could not see what all my excitement was about. And so she half-way peered through the clear place my nose had made on the window, then shook her head, hugged me close to her – and away we went to our car. (Which despite the fact it was running, had not run anywhere.) Into this nice, warm, cozy, going-to-drive away-pretty-soon-now car we went, both onto the crowded back seat, until Mom could dry the front seat, it having gotten snowed on so.

But Mom still didn't get it! And me having frantic-like tried my valiant best to explain to her why I did **not** want to drive away without making some monumental effort to obtain that girl-bear. Even telling her I'd noticed her nose was shaped just like mine! And didn't Mom think that was a good omen? Anything to break this impasse, which is a new word Mom just explained to me a few days ago, and means two people having completely different opinions about the same thing. Like, for example, the precious little girl-bear. And I guess I was over-excited, and suddenly couldn't talk very well – but then, who wouldn't be?!

Mom just shook her head and said "You can't just go in and take something out of that nice man's window, Charlie. We'd have to pay him for her, for he's in business to make money. And I just don't have very much money left after that extravagant shopping I did, buying new clothes for myself." And several other comments, all in this same no money left context.

So I tried to tell her that I thought this money for bear exchange had maybe overtones of slavery. She then said that it wasn't like that at all, and tried to explain to me that she just didn't have any more cash with her, and her credit card was about at its limit.

"The prices at that shop, Charlie, are too high for me to pay. I just can't afford her now," Mom said, shaking her head and trying to get ready to drive home.

I was in absolute despair, for by this time Mom had wrapped me up in a blanket, from which I couldn't get loose. Not only that, I was just about buried under those packages which contained Mom's so-called extravagances (but which sure looked like clothes to me).

Suddenly, a few clear notes floated through the air, and heaven-inspired words found themselves coming from my quivering mouth. When I told Mom that she had **her** mate for life, and this was my utmost desire too, she finally understood what I was trying to say. Mom knew how much she and Father loved each other, and how much that awful yearning sweeps over people. Suddenly Mom got tears in her eyes, and looked at me, nodding her head.

"Even though you haven't even met her yet, Charlie, you think she is your own true love?" she asked me.

"Please Mom," I begged, something wet suddenly dripping from my gold eyes onto my beautiful, new, forever-awaited, matchey-all-over gold suit onto which snow had already gotten. My lip quivered more.

"Charlie! You're crying **tears**!" Mom said, astonished, as she removed me from my blanket and tried to comfort me.

Finally Mom put me down, picked up her purse, and said "Maybe I can horse-swap him for the girl bear." I don't really understand what horses have to do with getting my love, but I looked at Mom's **determined** expression and felt a ray of hope.

I didn't know what on earth my Mom might have that the man didn't have and might want, him having such an absolutely crammed-full shop of uninteresting stuff I couldn't imagine anybody could want. Just old things. (Outside of that beautiful girl-bear.)

Finally, my resourceful Mom, said something like "Now, you just leave it to me, Charlie. I'm not my Father's daughter for nothing. I've really got a proclivity for this sort of horse-swapping!" There was that expression again.

And she muttered a few more things to herself about a Toby Mug, and some Bennington Ware and, while it broke her heart to think of parting with them, she could see my heart was breaking.

She rummaged around in her disorganated purse-thing, which evidently had a lot of things which were not appropriate in this horse-swapping deal. Including some T bags and part of a candy bar she had forgotten to finish eating. But Mom looked rather surprised when she did find a fair amount of what sure looked like cash to me, but what she called green stuff – and with that in her hand, she took off for the shop.

I just sat there with goosebumps, both from having been so cold in the snow – and heart-aching goosebumps, because I understood now, how a heart-stopping ache can make goosebumps too.

In not too long a time – but which seemed absolutely **interminable** to me (and I finally understood the meaning of that long word I'd puzzled over since Mom used it so often) here came Mom, out of the shop, down the snowy steps – carefully – holding something I couldn't see, sheltered half-way under her coat.

But the outline under her coat looked so small! **Surely** it wasn't a substitute? **Surely** she couldn't have mistaken who I meant? **Surely!**

But it **was** my love, looking out from Mom's coat. Looking at me with her shy, downcast eyes. Looking almost as bewildered as **I** felt.

And Mom made room next to me in my blanket. And tenderly placed my love beside me. (And I know it may sound "hokey," which is another favorite expression of Father's, but I want to tell it to you anyways):

AND MY LOVE AND I RODE OFF INTO THE SUNSET ON OUR ROMANTIC WHITE HORSE!

Well, I don't know exactly how many horses Mom's white car has, or why "horse-swapping" had brought me my love.

I just know that my Mom **really** pulled off a deal. Somehow.

*Mom wrapped me and Merrybell carefully in a piece of red velvet
(which she says is the color of love)
so we could have a chance to further our acquaintanceship*

29

THINGS NOT TO SAY TO AN OLDER GIRL BEAR

Maybe you expected the Twenty-Eight Chapter to be the end.

After all, I didn't just get my beautiful, forever-awaited golden furwool suit, but Mom pulled off a miracle and got me Merrybell, my true love, to live with us forever. Which, to my way of understanding, is a long time. A VERY long time. With lots and lots of happiness in between.

For Merrybell **is** my love. She came to fill my heart, like one crystal-clear note, ringing merrily. That's what I told Mom when she asked where on earth the name came from. And Mom told Father, who replied with a smile, something like . . . "well, it **is** getting pretty crowded around here, but I guess there's always room for more **LOVE.**"

At first, when we got home, and Father opened his gentle brown eyes from a "good snooze," complete with lots of zizzly sounds, his eyes were slightly startled, then questioning, then resigned. To see another bear coming in with Charlie, wrapped in a blanket! He looked at mother and said, "Having bears around here is almost as bad as having rabbits." But Mom gave Father some sort of human hand signal, so he didn't say anything more until after Mom returned to the living room.

Mom hurried us to our room, and mis- (or is it dis-)placed Big Red and A.B. Rabbit onto another chair she cleared expeditiously so we could be alone. So we could talk things over and get acquainted and all kinds of highly important stuff, which you, as humans, probably already know about, but which Charlie, being an intelligent but semi-anteek, teddy bear, having lived in a dark cardboard box most of his life until Mom providentially rescued him and, having never been in love with a girl bear before, needed time to learn how to be proper in his new relationship. (And I 'spect that's another "too long" sentence, but I hope you understand.)

No sooner had Mom placed us on our chair than there arose a large problem.

No words at all from Merrybell; maybe a faint sigh of contentment as Mom unwrapped us and positioned us together on our chair, after removing that highly inappropriate lace hat.

Mom, thoughtful as always, wrapped Merrybell in a piece of beautiful velvet. Red – just like the color of love, Mom said. And I'd wanted to hold Merrybell's velvet paw, and give her some reassurances, but she was all wrapped up. Just like me in my stalwart Chieftain's brown blanket, before I got my suit.

Then Mom said "this is only temporary . . . and then I'll make her a really charming dress – and maybe a charming little hat to match!" When she said "before long," I smiled and thought "don't count on it!" Cause I know all about Mom's "before longs." But Mom means well, even if she hasn't been able to use that new, big bargain, special sewing machine she got after standing all one long, hot, bee-stinging day at a sale.

Anyway, while we were on our chair, I could smell delicious smells wafting from the kitchen, Father having surprised Mom by fixing one of his good Swiss-steaks with veggies . . . because he knew how tired Mom would be on account of all her shopping. And asking her what she'd been able to find. And Mom answering she hadn't found very much, but she had found a few real bargains.

But the food, as tantalizing as its smells were, didn't appeal to Charlie. And I wondered if maybe I was love-sick and had lost my appetite, like they say humans do. But since I have had no tears to come out of my eyes, except when I begged Mom to understand about Merrybell, and I haven't any intestines either (thank goodness for that!), I really didn't have to worry about my lack of interest in the food. Although I do like it very much when Mom lets me sit (stand actually, since I don't have knees) on a chair at their table and listen to all the truly fascinating human-type information Mom and Father share.

So I just stood there, not paying much attention to the food smells, just trying to look stalwart, and I put out my left arm in my finally appropriate golden suit, trying to shelter this small, bewildered-looking bear. And then I found that she wasn't so much bewildered, as maybe – **uninterested**? For I thought she moved over – away from Charlie – just the littlest bit. (Maybe to find her own space?) And I remembered Mom had told me, "We mustn't be concerned if she's shy at first, Charlie, because she's evidently been through a lot, and we'll just have to give her time."

So, trying to be helpful, I began to try to explain this time-stuff to Merrybell, and how I figured we maybe didn't have too much of it, what with me already being middle-aged and all. And, me not knowing anything about the life-span of teddy bears, said maybe she'd like to tell me how many years older she was than me? Well, **that** was a big mistake! Even I could see that, for Merrybell suddenly looked around at me with an almost fierce look in those previously gentle, bewildered eyes, and then she **really** moved over! Clear out of the encircling, loving arms of Charlie – who'd not known much about women, and so had evidently **really** put his foot in his mouth. (Which, of course, I hadn't figured I could do, me not having any knees.)

Mom and I had already discussed, very briefly (and because of her looking back over her shoulder in the car every once in a while to hear what I was carrying on so about from the back seat) that, even if this girl-bear was older than I was, I didn't care a rap about things like that. "After all," I said, "look at you and me, Mom!"

And Mom had not corrected me, for gosh sakes, or given me any indication of the things of utmost importance I must not say to older women! (In this case, older bear-women). So I was **really** dejected now, because here was Merrybell and Charlie, alone, on our chair in Mom's and my room (Mom having just moved Big Red and A.B. Rabbit to another spot so Merrybell and Charlie could have time to further our acquaintanceship), and I couldn't figure out what to do. About anything.

But then a providential thing happened, for I had what I thought must be a brilliant idea. Because I'd heard Mom explaining about "anteeks" several times, and saying she didn't think I could be an anteek, since she figured I was only about fifty-two (or was that sixty-two), or something, counting back to when I'd been borned around the 1940's War.

And from that, I thought I'd been able to tell . . . that there was maybe some dividing line of this anteek stuff – like maybe authentically having to be over one-hundred?? And since I couldn't count nearly that far, and knew authentic meant being more valuable,

I tried to arrange things in their rightful context. And presented this elucidating fact to Merrybell, just in case she was a true anteek, or at least an **almost** one, her being older than Charlie. Which she evidently didn't think being a valuable anteek was any better than the other reassuring things I'd tried to tell her. Maybe, not even as much.

Well, I decided this was one of those times when I'd better keep my mouth shut. And I did. And then, with a sideways glance at me – quickly concealed – Merrybell looked from me to some of Mom's paintings on the walls (and tried to act uninterested). Suddenly just two or three beautiful musical "signs" came out of her mouth! With great similarity to some of the ones we'd heard at friend Barbara's, floating out from Uncle Ben's smiley mouth!

And I knew then what was the matter: I HADN'T BEEN SPEAKING HER LANGUAGE!

But I was encouraged, although I didn't understand Merrybell's sounds any better than the ones Uncle Ben had made. And then a few more sounds, or signs, or notes, or something – came floating out. And suddenly I thought Merrybell maybe looked frightened.

About this time, supper being over, Mom and Father suddenly stuck their heads in our door. And here came another sound or two from Merrybell.

Father got this tremendously astounded look on his face and said: "I thought you were teasing me, Mom, when you told me some of your stuffed animals could talk! Why, that new little girl bear is speaking German!"

Mom turned and looked at him and asked how on earth he knew that. Father said he'd studied German, as well as French, in college . . . didn't have much use for it . . . so he'd gotten sort of rusty. But he would recognize those words anywhere!

Mom asked him what they meant. And Father got this real sad look on his face, and said he'd . . . tell her later. And turned around kind of quiet-like, and left.

Well, Charlie knew – indubitably – that what Merrybell had just told Father was highly important. But Charlie also knew this was something to discuss privately with Mom. Not with Merrybell present. No more "put his foot in his mouth for Charlie" with Merrybell!

So all through that evening, as we sort of cuddled together (no, I'll have to be honest, more like me cuddled, Merrybell aloof) I could hear fragments of Mom and Father's conversation coming from the other room. But I couldn't understand what they were saying.

And it was an **interminable** night. For my heart was filled with longing, trying to establish some sort of rapport with my love.

But from somewhere in my dreams, I heard those faint, melodic, flying-away-to-find-love notes.

30

BIG HE-MONGOUS SURPRISES

"Charlie!" Mom gasped, as she found my present to her under the tree that big, momentous Christmas holiday after Merrybell came into my life. "However did you accomplish this?"

Well, I didn't want to tell her, not right away at least because Charlie, for once, had done something really special for his Mom – and Father too – and I didn't want to give away how exactly it was I had pulled off such a surprise.

It had already been a magical holiday season – no little persons trying to grab Charlie or Merrybell by their tender ears. Big Red being as near speechless as I had ever seen him when Santa brought him a special I.U. flag thing (Mom says it's called a pennant) to wave during I.U. basketball games. And under our tree, in a pretty box – another momentous surprise – my friend **SQUIRRELY!** Wearing a handsome Christmas vest -- and a new tail! Mom smiled when she saw how pleased I was, and said the "Doll Lady" had worked a miracle on him, to which I agreed indubitably!

This year Mom and Father managed to place the holiday decorations so that the cats (three now, Big Boy having moved inside, even though he has lots of heavy pelage to protect him outside from the cold) couldn't break them like before. Once again there were twinkling golden lights on the tall Hemlock trees just outside our front windows.

More special lights: the Menorrah with its white candles lighted, red candles glowing in genuine anteek brass sticks Mom's grandmother had left her.

Lots of little presents and hugs to and from friends dropping by.

Big, **huge** surprises for both Charlie and Merrybell – Charlie getting really neat, special shiny black boots with some kind of dressy (there's that word again) white socks with tiny buttons on them. No more old worn black feet showing! Mom said the special socks were actually called "spats" (which I thought had something to do with fights), and were for "special occasions" when I wear my stalwart Scots tar-tan outfit. Incidentally, Merrybell told me she loves my new boots and "spats." She says they make me look "very handsome." So maybe Charlie has been wrong in thinking the suit "inappropriate."

Charlie even got a **second** pair of little boots, "work boots," Mom said, these to wear while helping Mom and Father in our gardens. Which Father is already planning. Ideas for this year's gardens drawn and labeled. All neat and organized.

And for Merrybell? One of Mom's dearest friends had lovingly sewn a beautiful red velvet dress for her to give Merrybell, so now she has two special dresses – another friend having made her a pretty long dress, which Mom says is quilted anteek rose satin. But Mom and I agree not to mention the word "anteek" to Merrybell ever again, her still being highly sensitive to something that doesn't change Charlie's love for his Merrybell one whit.

And with these dresses, my love now wears a golden chain with a sparkling gem, gift of Uncle Ben, who friend Barbara and Stephen brought from the Nursey Home for a special visit at Christmas.

It seems that funny looking gold button thing which was in the pocket of my awful girl's dress, was an important ancient gold coin.

Though how it ever got in my pocket we'll never know! Anyway, in between all the other beautiful sounds which still came when Uncle Ben tried to speak, friend Barbara said Uncle Ben knew it was an important "artifact," and wanted to donate it to one of the museums where he had worked.

But Charlie has been so excited telling you about everything else special that happened this Christmas, he almost forgot to tell you about the **big**, momentous, surprise Christmas present he gave his Mom. And Father too. For when Mom opened the package (youngest daughter having helped Charlie wrap his gift beautifully), here was a photo of Charlie, with his most stalwart, steadfast expression, with little baby sheeps all around him. It was framed special, and oldest daughter had helped Charlie sign his picture with his golden paw pressed on a stamp pad.

"Oh, Charlie!" Mom exclaimed. "However did you accomplish this?" And then she picked Charlie up, and gave him lots and lots of yummy hugs, only stopping when I gave a slight lift of my eyebrow towards my Merrybell. I knew Mom would understand and, sure enough, she did! Picking Merrybell up tenderly – so as not to startle her – she shared special hugs with Merrybell too.

"Merry Christmas, Merrybell," Mom said. "Welcome to our family."

And I thought I heard another sigh of contentment from my love.

*I asked my Mom, was my blue and white outfit
(which sure looks like doll jammies to me)
appropriate to wear for her highly important birthday picture*

Father with Sammy Siamese, him being another rescue cat which Father found and brought home

A Bear Called Charlie 163

Charlie's BIG HE-MONGOUS *Christmas present for his Mom (and Father too), determined to look his stalwart best in his photo with the little sheeps*

Me in my stalwart Scots Chieftain tar-tan suit, with Merrybell, my true love, Big Red, Beaner and Squirrely

31

THE INEVITABILITY OF THE MATTER

"Is Heaven a long time, Mom?" I asked one snowy evening. She had been reading to me and Merrybell in front of the fireplace. "Longer than Squirrely and I got stuck in the cardboard box in Sally's grandmother's attic?"

She put down her book and looked at me quizzical-like. "Heaven is **forever**, Charlie," she said. "Why do you ask?"

"Because the story you've been reading us really makes me think about Father, and how much I miss him. And even the two ancient cats." Charlie paused for a moment. "I know it's been a long time since they died, but I still think about Father every day. And all the happifying things we got to do together . . . and his dear little zizzly sounds when he slept . . . and how he got everything all organized and neat and tidy. And how much love there was in our house." I felt big tears start to run down to my insides.

About then Big Boy, who was now himself indubitably in process of becoming a semi-anteek cat, got up from where he had been snoozing, and came over to me, smooshing Charlie with a loving nudge plus a great big smoochy kiss, before finally transferring his gigantic, heavily pelaged body to Mom's lap. And that made Charlie think about his best cat friend, Patches who, Mom says, is in Heaven with Father because some expletive expletive human type person deliberately poisoned her. And everybody cried 'cause she was such a sweet girl kitty.

"And I'm worried about you, Mom," I said finally, my lip quivering in spite of the fact I was trying always to be my most stalwart best for my Mom and Merrybell.

"Worried about me?" Mom asked, looking surprised.

I nodded.

'Cause I'm most probably now a nearly anteek bear, and you're getting older, and . . . . " And I gave a tiny little lift of my eyebrow toward my Merrybell, her still being highly sensitive about being older than Charlie. "And sometimes, Mom, you talk about 'flying away,' and I get scared."

About that time she rearranged Big Boy a little on her lap, so she would have space to share her lap with me too. But first she gave me a **he-mongous**, yummy hug, and the most beautiful smile came on her face, as she patted my extraordinarily handsome golden head.

"Oh, Charlie!" Mom said. "What joy you have brought to my life!" Smiling, she gave Charlie what she calls a "love pat."

"Everybody dies sometime, Charlie, and most of the time people don't know when that will happen. Which is why, I have told you before, it is **very** important to treat each day as if it could be your last on this beautiful earth, and try to leave the world a better place than it was when you were born."

Well, boy! If **anyone** had done that, it was certainly my Mom and Father. All the hurt and injured little animals Father had rescued and cared for. And made sure they had extra special good homes before he let the people adopt them. And the way he made people smile at the Nursey Home when we went to visit. And how many people he and Mom helped learn to read in a special program at the learned tomes library. Even the trees and flowers in our yard practically smiled when Father took care of them, because he made them even more beautiful. Father was **very** respectful of nature type things.

And my **Mom!** No one had to tell Charlie just how special she was, 'cause I knew that indubitably. I was so lucky that Mom had saved me at that dreadful auction all those years ago. And brought Charlie to live with her and Father and the two ancient cats, in our beautiful home. And had rescued my Merrybell too. And had made her feel safe – and loved by **all** our family. Not just Charlie. Who loved her most of all, of course.

And Father had even taken time from his highly important work to learn all about the traumas my Merrybell had suffered because of the War Effort, when she was a young girl bear in Germany. Father told Mom, when he was able to translate her worried German sounds better – that all of her family was killed a long time ago, because of some very expletive evil men. And my love suffered terrible traumas, and had no family and no friends left where she felt safe and could hide. And got sold, along with everything else in her home, by thieves who stole everything and sold it, not caring that my love's family had been murdered.

And somehow Merrybell ended up in a great big metal box type thing called a shipping container, and came on a great big boat to America. And no one wanted to buy her, and give her a nice home like Charlie had, because she was so little. And people said hurtful things in front of her about her being "insignificant" and too expensive. So my Merrybell sat in first one anteek store, then another, being traded from place to place. For even longer than Charlie and Squirrely had been stuck in their box in the dark attic. And she was all alone and frightened and sad. Til my Mom helped Charlie rescue his love that big**,** momentous day.

Everyone told Charlie how special his Mom was. (Well, not exactly **told** Charlie, because people didn't realize I was one highly intelligent bear who could speak and listen carefully, and who had even written this book – with Mom's help, for sure). And was now even writing a learned tomes dictionary for teddy bears, to help them understand Human-speak better. So I listened quietly and understood all the good things people said about my Mom.

Even though Charlie was now finally able to understand lots of important numbers, and had worked very hard to be able to count to one hundred – almost – he still had problems with those tricky wunz and trews. So, this being a problem, Charlie cannot say exactly how many people Mom has helped since she adopted Charlie. Only that there were big, momentous numbers of them. And it made Charlie smile because everyone felt happified when they spoke to his Mom.

Cause she was wise. Very, very wise.

So I guess my Mom is right when she says I shouldn't worry about God having any space in Heaven for bears like Charlie and his Merrybell. And Big Red and Squirrely too. And we probably still have lots more time to do good things, and learn lots more highly important stuff right here on earth before we fly away on our next true life adventure, with my Mom.

And I felt all warm and loved and wanted when Mom said that to me. And decided to just settle down to the inevitability of the matter.

*I know I am one LUCKY bear to have been rescued by my Mom,
who loves me and even rescued my Merrybell.*

32

THE CORD OF LOVE

Then, finally, I knew what "The Signs" were!

I'd had such trouble identifying them, for they were spun from dreams – fragile as the golden threads of Charlie's suit.

And as they melded, I realized that they were the knowledge accumulated in my lifetime. I'd become wise enough to understand they were all the kind things people had said to me when I'd needed them.

They were Love and Sharing, Compassion and Kindness, Forbearance and Trust. Every good thing I'd experienced in my lifetime of searching.

Then I wondered how I could ever explain them to anyone else, and knew I needn't worry. For the Cord of Love – though invisible – connects us all.

Author

EPILOGUE

It proved to be our final Christmas together. We spent the day lost in the memories of so many magical holidays before, inhaling the moments of those now silenced conversations, remembering the presents lovingly made or purchased and placed beneath the trees, the sounds and scents of all the blessings our family had enjoyed.

Then, inevitably, one by one our tiny family disappeared: first, each of our two remarkable grandmothers, then, one by one our wonderful aunts and uncles, my extraordinarily caring Father, and most recently, my beloved Joseph.

"Can you believe they're all gone?" Mom said suddenly, in the midst of yet another Scrabble game, a favorite pastime of ours. Putting down her tiles for a moment, she took my hands in hers, kissed them both. "I suspect it won't be long before I fly away too."

Suddenly, I was nearly blinded by tears. Sure, she was now in her nineties, and had physically slowed down greatly these last two years. But mentally? She was sharp as a tack, a voracious reader, determined to help Charlie finish this memoir. Besides, her own mother had been almost 97 when she died, and our great grandmother had been 103.

I looked at Charlie, standing at full alert on the table between us, trying to understand our every move when we played Scrabble. Charlie frequently told us how much he loved "participating" in our game, earnestly committed to understanding the endless peculiarities of human language. I saw a tiny lift of his brow, a quiver of his lower lip as he looked at Mom and me with those forever mesmerizing gold eyes of his.

Mom saw it too.

"I'm fine, Charlie," she said reassuringly, smiling.

"I'm just old."

Mom died exactly as she had wanted: in her bedroom, propped up in her bed so she could enjoy the quickly reinstalled twinkling Christmas lights and the birds flitting close by after a feeder was moved closer for her to enjoy.

She was surrounded by her paintings, her favorite books, her typewriter and notes nearby, along with her assemblage of beloved stuffed animals. Charlie and Merrybell lay close beside her, and she smiled as she looked one more time at Charlie, now resplendent as a stalwart Scots chieftain, his outfit lovingly created and sewn piece by piece by Mom during the last few years.

And then, with a gentle whisper of angel wings, she was gone.

"Isn't it time for us to fly away with Mom?" Charlie asked as I returned from her funeral. I picked him up and held him close, just as I had so many times before. He smelled just like Mom.

"No, Charlie," I finally managed to say. "Remember what we promised Mom last Christmas?" A fresh wave of grief washed over me. "You and Merrybell and all your furry friends are coming to live with me. It's going to be a whole new adventure for you."

Charlie refused to be deterred. "But she's my now and forever Mom," Charlie said, persisting, "and she promised we would always be together." He paused. "And my Merrybell too, of course."

"She's my now and forever Mom too, Charlie. And we **will** be together again someday. But you and I are younger than Mom, and we still have important things to do before it's our time to fly away. Besides," I said, "people are going to want to meet you once your book is published."

"But there're lots more important and valuable teddy bears in the world than Charlie," he said, insistent.

"And I know," he said continuing, "even though everyone told Mom how handsome Charlie is in his golden furwool suit, and my stalwart Scots chieftain tar-tan, I'm still just an almost anteek 15" teddy bear made from cheap red flannel with old black feet. And no knees."

"No, Charlie." I held him close to me. "That's not what you are at all." I smiled as I looked at him again.

"I'm not?" Charlie asked, surprised.

I shook my head and hugged him.

"Somehow, Charlie, in the process of your being highly motivated and absolutely **determinated** to become erudite so our Mom would be even prouder of you than she already was, you have become what Father called a 'Fur Person.' That's what you are, Charlie," I said, smiling, the scent of Mom permeating the air that enveloped us both.

Charlie's eyes widened.

"A Fur Person?" He asked.

I nodded.

"And I suspect, Charlie, that makes you one of the rarest and wisest teddy bears in the entire world."

ACKNOWLEDGEMENTS

I wish to express my gratitude to two of mother's closest friends, Laura Bybee and Sophia Hauserman, for their thoughtful suggestions about the manuscript following our mother's death.

I wish also to acknowledge the invaluable suggestions of our neighbors and friends, Barry and Barbara Knister, as Charlie and I worked diligently to insure that our mother's dream – this memoir – would come to fruition. May it bring as much happiness to countless readers, as it has to us.

Special thanks also to our close friends, Wanda and Jack Mayo, and their wonderful golden lab, Maxwell Smart Mayo. In addition to the boundless energy and unending antics of my own family of rescued cats, Maxwell and his four-legged best friends, Precious Biggs and Duncan Hogan, along with Chelsea Knister, have provided me with much needed levity during the emotionally difficult past few months.

Thanks also to my sister, Madi Arnett, my niece, Diana Markland, and friends Judi Medalen, Fran Miller, Bea Jackson, Marlene Levin, Sandra Yeyati, Dianne Sponseller, Charles Sobczek, Amos Simon and Elena Diamante (who remains the principal advocate for equal photo ops for Squirrely).

Finally, I am forever grateful to the unknown persons who discarded Charlie, Squirrely and Merrybell. Thank you for freeing each of them to be rescued and become much loved, full-fledged members of our family.

Peg Goldberg Longstreth

Gold Mountain Press
Mission Statement

Apple CEO and co-founder, Steve Jobs, is on record as saying people no longer read. **Gold Mountain Press** was founded to prove him wrong.

We believe readers are waiting for books that respect human intelligence, that are engaging and accessible without being dumbed down. In short, the mission of **Gold Mountain Press** is to publish works of fiction and non-fiction that will speak to the human condition, and thereby meet the intelligent reader's wish to be inspired and informed.

"If you build it, he will come," says a character in the film *Field of Dreams*. **Gold Mountain Press** believes this idea relates to literature. If you build better books, people will come, and they will read.

GOLD MOUNTAIN PRESS

Gold Mountain Press
5640 Taylor Road, Suite D4
Naples, Florida 34109
www.goldmountainpress.com